UPCOMING
TALES OF THE FORGOTTEN GOD
BY DAN HAMILTON

THE CHAMELEON LADY
THE EVERLASTING CHILD

TALES OF THE FORGOTTEN GOD

THE BEGGAR KING

Dan Hamilton

Illustrated by
Jack Stockman

INTERVARSITY PRESS
DOWNERS GROVE, ILLINOIS 60515

InterVarsity Press® is the book-publishing division of InterVarsity Christian Fellowship®, a student
movement active on campus at hundreds of universities, colleges and schools of nursing in the United
States of America, and a member movement of the International Fellowship of Evangelical Students. For
information about local and regional activities, write Public Relations Dept., InterVarsity Christian
Fellowship, 6400 Schroeder Rd., P.O. Box 7895, Madison, WI 53707-7895.

Cover art: Jack Stockman

ISBN 0-8308-1671-2

Printed in the United States of America ∞

Library of Congress Cataloging-in-Publication Data

Hamilton, Dan.
    The beggar king/Dan Hamilton.
      p.   cm.—(Tales of the forgotten God)
    ISBN 0-8308-1671-2
    I. Title. II. Series.
    PS3558.A4248B4 1993
    813'.54—dc20   93-19200
                                    CIP

| 16 | 15 | 14 | 13 | 12 | 11 | 10 | 9 | 8 | 7 | 6 | 5 | 4 | 3 | 2 | 1 |
| 05 | 04 | 03 | 02 | 01 | 00 | 99 | 98 | 97 | 96 | 95 | 94 | 93 | | | |

—CONTENTS—

1/The Dead of Night _____ 9

2/A Night for Names _____ 18

3/The Lion of the Hills _____ 26

4/After the Rain _____ 35

5/Trial by Fire _____ 44

6/Trial Without Fire _____ 58

7/This Shall Be My House _____ 68

8/The Book & the Burden _____ 77

9/Proven Metal _____ 83

10/The Woes of the World _____ 86

11/The Bright Flower _____ 91

12/The Wondrous Wine _____ 95

13/Before Winter _____ 102

14/A Price of Tears _____ 106

15/Words for the Wounded _____ 112

16/The Hope of the Healer _____ 115

17/Beauty & the Feast _____ 120

18/The Marvelous Mirror _____ 132

19/The Five Windows _____ 137

20/Old Promises _____ 144

ONE

The
Dead of
Night

Here in the highlands the winter grain was ripe for harvest. Spring had begun to bring warm days, but the nights were still cold and sometimes frosty. And this spring midnight clung to the village like an old woolen blanket, shutting out the world and muffling the sounds that might otherwise have drifted from house to house within the village walls.

An old woman huddled alone and sleepless by the smoldering fire in the village square, gazing long into the darkness, seeing nothing and noticing less. But she roused at the creak of iron gates and the sound of slow footfalls clear but soft in the silence. She waited, looking toward the western gate of the village. A man came walking there, his faint shadow leaning before him, away from the bright moon at his back. Drawing near into the dim light of the all-night fire, he slowly shifted from a black silhouette into a dusty beggar wrapped in a stained cloak and sheltered under the weary brim of an ancient, shapeless hat. His steps betrayed the knowledge that his feet had endured too many miles, and that perhaps his blisters had not yet turned to calluses.

The beggar stopped before the woman and peered at her, as though surprised to see her alone and awake in the depths of the night. She bade him welcome, and he asked where he might find food and a corner in which to sleep.

"There is no more food to be had," she said, "for it has all been bought and laid aside for the stranger who gives life to the dead. And no room either, for all places have been claimed in hope that the stranger will tarry here."

The beggar collapsed wearily on the stone paving. His voice held a note of interest that denied the hour and his fatigue. "Tell me of this stranger," he asked.

She was silent for a space, groping in the close darkness for words. Then she began in a low tone, curiously numb and flat. "We heard first the tales from another village—word of a tall man in white who raised the dead to life and gave away gold while voices sang in the sky. And that he left under the mid-day sun, mounted on a white charger with a harness of gold and bells of silver. Heading south, it was said, and perhaps on his way to this very village." She paused, shifted restlessly, and sighed before going on. "So the rumors said. All our people purchased fine food to store in hope, gathered gold to lay at the stranger's feet, and made ready rooms to house the healer. They prepared for him and lined the road beyond the north gate to await him. You see, death is no new visitor here. Red plagues and old age and wild beasts have all helped fill the graveyard within the walls of this village. I cannot blame the people for their dreams, though I did not join them. Their hope lies only in new things revealed.

"But no stranger came that day or the next. Some crept back to their houses. Some feared that he would never come and that they would never find their blessing. Those who wield power still sought the right to host the stranger and lay their dead at his feet.

"Then yesterday there was dust on the horizon, and a man came riding—a tall man in a white robe on a white stallion, with a harness trimmed in silver and gold. The crowds surged to meet him, cheering, pleading, and all but bore him under. He lifted his voice, but no one could have heard him. They brought him here to the square, where our richest man had placed the body of his eldest son, slain in a wine-sotted brawl over the affections of a woman. The stranger stood bewildered next to the body, and he asked the people what they wanted of him.

"They demanded that he raise the dead man, to do the wonders he had done in other towns. He replied that his name was Candolel, that he was not a god but a merchant, and that the power of life rested not in his hands." She paused for a long moment, and the heaviness of her heart was betrayed by the words she did not say.

She drew a long shuddering breath and continued. "He denied that he was their desire, so they killed him. They pulled him down in their rage, and beat him, and left him dead in the square.

"At least, so these things were told to me, for I came only in time to find two dead men here. And now the people have returned to their houses to wait until the true healer comes. Perhaps some of them are afraid of what they have done, but they bear their guilt lightly."

The beggar was silent while the woman gazed at his faded cloak and sore feet and weary limbs. "This town, like others," she added, "is not overkind to beggars. But I, too, have wandered and sought the favor of those unknown to me, and so I will not despise you. Yet, I am only an old woman, and I have nothing that anyone—even you—would covet. My hut is not far from here. I can offer you little but stale bread, well water, and a place to bathe your feet. I have an old stable where my donkey sleeps, and you may put his straw under your head for a pillow. It is little enough, but I offer it to you freely."

He thanked her quietly. And then they rose, and she led him slowly through the town.

"I am Abra," she said over her shoulder. "I am the outcast."

"Call me Covenant," he responded. "I am the king of beggars."

Their voices barely bruised the hush of the empty streets. They passed under the stone arch with its squeaking gates.

"There is no watchman here," she told him. "These gates are here to keep the wild animals out." She brandished her walking stick at the shadows, adding, "But if you travel alone, you clearly are not afraid of them."

"No, I am not."

"Then what are you afraid of?"

"I am afraid of nothing, but I believe that the greatest dangers are the beasts that live within the walls."

She nodded grimly, and they passed out along a lonely pathway. She pointed to a grove of trees near at hand. "Candolel is buried there."

"Who buried him?"

"I did."

"I see two fresh graves there. Is there not a graveyard within the walls of the village?"

She did not answer him, though fresh tears came to her eyes. They walked on, and he let her silence stand unchallenged. In that same silence, they reached her dwelling. There, she tended his torn feet while he sat in a pile of soft rushes. Later, she divided her portion of bread with him.

"Woman," the beggar said softly, "your eyes betray their sadness. You may weep before me without fear, for I speak the language of those who grieve." Then her hidden river of tears spilled over its banks, and she wept, and spoke to him of her daughter, dead a fortnight, taken by the red sickness that had clawed the village.

"Your only child?"

She nodded.

"And she sleeps in that second grave, does she not?"

She nodded again.

"Why is she not buried within the walls? And why is not Candolel, for that matter?"

"Because I am still a stranger here, even after many years; my fathers did not live here before me. The village is only for those who have been here forever. So it is I who must dwell out here and Kali who must sleep in unhallowed ground. As for Candolel, the village is not worthy to hold his grave."

He stared into the decrepit hearth at the tiny fire that held back the sting of the night. "Forgive me if I renew your grief. This stranger—Candolel—why did you give your care to him? Not even kind women bury strangers in hallowed places, places where old, deep love lies sleeping."

"Twelvemonth ago . . . twelvemonth ago Candolel was found near this village, a traveler wounded and stripped by thieves. The people ignored him, and he recovered here in this cottage. Kali tended him. In time, he chose her for himself, and she him, with my blessing. Then he left for the great town called Glory to deal there and regain his fortune. He came once again with a pledge for Kali, and then promised to return for us both when wealth was again fully his, when he could ride proudly through the village and let the people gawk as he came to us and brought favor to a house of outcasts. That would have ended our sorrow here, and we would have returned with him to Glory."

"Why does Glory draw you so?" the beggar asked. "What lies there?"

"Where else but Glory? Where else might one find kings and palaces, fountains and magic stones? All *this*," she said, sweeping her arms wide, "is a vacant land with but a single jewel in it: Glory! It is a place of many great secrets."

"And at least one great secret it has forgotten it has," smiled the beggar.

"A new life—an end to hardship," she continued, unhearing, as though lost in a dream. "I have never been there—but Candolel has . . . had been. It is truly great, and a place of dreams fulfilled. All who live there have riches and a name.

"But does it matter now what is there?" she continued, not expecting an answer as she stoked the fire and wiped strands of hair from her tear-soaked face. "Without Candolel and without Kali, I have no hope of Glory."

"There are other ways to enter Glory than in splendor, and other ways to live than to be served."

The woman turned from the fire and looked at her guest, but did not answer. He waved a hand back along the path toward the willow grove. "Twofold is your right to sorrow, and yet you do not seek the gifts of the coming stranger?"

"No! I fear him! If he holds power over the grave, he is not a man but a god come among us. And if a god, then terrible is the price he may demand in exchange for healing, and more terrible yet his wrath if we presume upon him. No," she said, shaking her head, "I pray only that he will pass us by."

"Yet all your hope lies buried in the dark embrace of the earth," said the beggar. "Even if the lifegiver walked here tonight, you would not seek his favor?"

"No," she replied, sinking onto a low stool by the hearth. "I will not, nor could I even draw near because of the people who claim higher rights—and back their claims with hammered gold. And what could I sacrifice to him? My donkey?" She laughed, but there was little humor in it. "Even the most miserable god would reject that offering. And I have neither gold nor silver. Yet, I do wish that I might dare to brave the power of the gods. But better is the death that comes to all people than the destruction that comes upon fools."

"If this stranger throws coins to the needy, why should he be tempted by gold and silver? And if he is drawn to you by

praise and fame, why does no one know his name?"

She had no ready answer.

"Why do you even believe that this stranger will come?" he persisted. "Or that he holds power from on high? Perhaps he is only a rumor."

"If the old stories are true," she replied, "then he is a *promise* and not merely a *rumor*."

"The old stories?" the beggar prompted, relaxing in his pile of rushes as though he were settling to hear a long tale.

"The old stories," she repeated, "of the Elder God and the Lost City."

"I have not heard some of those tales for many years. Please tell me again, that I may have them afresh."

"I have not heard the words since I was a little girl," she replied, "but I have forgotten none of them." She paused, remembering. "In my village, an old man would sit late before the fire, and I would come to sit beside him and listen to his words in the darkness." She recited the words shyly but readily, as if she had often said them silently in her heart. "Once, there was the City," she began, using the ancient pattern, "where dwelt the Elder God and all the men and women and children he had made. All shone, all had joy, and all were loved. The City was full of life and wonders and trees with fruit good to eat, and the Elder God walked among them and dwelt in their midst.

"A great wall surrounded the City, and in the walls were many gates. But beyond the gates lay the wilderness—forbidden to all, though left open to their feet—and at each gate was a path that led winding into the wilderness. Although the gates had been fashioned by the Elder God and marked with his warnings, the avenues beyond were made by his ancient enemy, who hated all good things everywhere. And that same one sang a haunting song in the distance, beckoning the curious on.

"All that the City dwellers needed was given them freely by

the Elder God, but they were not content as long as the un-
trodden paths to the unexplored wilderness shimmered in the
sun. One by one, boldly, or sharing their indecision in groups,
they ventured out onto the narrow paths to see what lay
beyond. The Elder God called after them and pleaded with
them, but their curiosity deafened their ears to his voice. And
from there they vanished. None ever returned. And even
though none of those who left ever returned to the City, the
people there still wondered about the wilderness. They said to
themselves that it must be wondrous indeed if the adventur-
ers chose it over the City. So they too went into the face of
the silence, and vanished. Soon they were all gone, and the
City stood empty."

"What happened to those who left?" the beggar asked softly, as if continuing an old ritual.

"First, the wilderness lay before them, then beside them on
either hand, and then it surrounded them. And the wilderness
terrified them, for there were lions there, and wolves, and
fierce things that lived in the sea. Darkness fell upon them,
and rain and thunder, and the world was changed in a great
shaking and windstorm; the people turned, but could not find
their way back to the City." She hesitated, and her pause
covered long measures of unspoken time. "After many years
of wandering, Glory was built as a reminder and a memorial,
hoping that the Elder God would return to them there. But
he has not. Even today the City is still lost, and the Elder God
has forgotten us."

Her voice trailed off into the night, as exhausted as her thin
frame.

TWO

A Night for Names

T HE BEGGAR TURNED TO HIS HOST AND REPLIED, "WHAT YOU have heard is true, but you have not heard all the truth. The City itself was never lost; it was *abandoned*. The Elder God removed it to a safe place, until the time comes for its streets to be walked again. It is humanity that is lost, and the path back to the City that is forfeited. The City is still the center of all the universe, and there the Elder God still reigns in unapproachable holiness. The City has a heart, and that heart has a name, and that name beats at the core of the earth, and clocks the candling of the stars.

"And the Elder God is not forgetting, but forgotten; not the forsaker, but the forsaken; not the abandoner, but the abandoned—not the one who is sought, but the one who seeks.

"Those who departed did not come back, for they could not:

the path betrayed them. It was not like other roads, for it was not made, but only suffered, by the Elder God. He himself had promised them that he would make them roads and highways through the wilderness, so that all the treasures yet to be discovered would be theirs as well as the City. Had they trusted him, his roads would soon have been under their feet to wander, and the roads would have been theirs to explore, and the wonders beyond theirs to conquer. But they did not wait until they had been tested, approved and empowered. Instead, they went in their own strength, and it was the wilderness that conquered them. It is still called the Lost City," he noted, "though it is not the City which is lost, but people who are still lost in the wilderness."

The flames crackled. She was silent, and he continued. "Glory was built as an echo, where they believed the City had been, yet Glory is only a well-meant but wicked and hopeless shadow of the City that was lost. They made themselves a king, to remind them of the Elder God. Since that time, we have lost count of the years, yet Glory has endured. And although kings still are crowned, the memory of the Elder God has faded from the land. Still, in no place is he altogether without a witness."

"I do not know if the Elder God is real or not. I hope that he is."

"You know more than you think, and you think more than you say. Why do you think the people walked away from the City?" the beggar asked. His voice was still soft, but it no longer carried the tones of the ritual.

"I don't know. I know only my own heart. I know that we are hopelessly human."

"You are human, but not as hopeless as you think. One may have hope, and never know it."

She stirred the fire with one hand before she responded. "Some say there is still a secret door, and behind it a dark and dangerous path to the City, winding its way back if only one could plumb its mysteries. But if there is a door leading to such a path, it is hidden, and no one knows where it is. So I was told by my forebears, who were told by theirs, whose own fathers had lived in the City."

"Only the Elder God can make such a thing—and all will remain lost in the wilderness until he comes to find them or sends one from the City to open the road of return."

"Such a one has been promised. He has not come."

"Perhaps he has—and you have not yet learned to recognize him." After a moment of thoughtful silence, the beggar stood. "We have talked much," he said. "You think you know who I am, but despair clouds your certainty. You have believed without seeing. Now there is something that you must see, for I do not think you can see without increasing your belief."

He took her arm and guided her outdoors through quiet fields, letting the moonlight embrace her sorrow. Bats joined them overhead, then flicked away into the blue-black bowl of the universe. Stars glimmered everywhere above, granting light but no warmth.

The beggar led her at last to the graves beneath the weeping trees. "You fear the dark gods," he said, "but there is One who is not dark. I know you have not forgotten the Elder God. But are you willing to trust the One who savors love and not the smell of smoke or sacrifice, who treasures the spread of mercy above the cold clink of coins? One who would not despise the gift of a donkey? One who knows that cold water may restore what fine wine cannot, that stale bread may give life where silver bars fail? He has long known your longings and your hopes. And for your faithful hopes and your kindness he has already ransomed your dead."

He turned to her. "What does this earth hold? Candolel? Kali? Perhaps not." She stared at him as he spread his arms above the double mounds. "Come, children!" he commanded, and there came a shudder in the darkness, a ripple of reluctant earth, twin convulsions beneath the grass. From the cold wombs of the graves, the reborn burst forth in an explosion of disregarded dirt. Abra, first silent with fright, then weeping with wild joy, embraced her daughter, then Candolel, then the beggar, and then all three. Love renewed by love renewed the chill air.

At last, the beggar urged them all toward the hut and the waiting fire.

"Go to your home," the beggar said, "and I shall return to you there. I have one last task to perform before we all leave this village behind. No longer will you forget the Elder God, for you shall indeed enter Glory—but in his name and not in your own. Return to your home now, all of you, and tell no one."

"Who is there to tell?" asked Abra. "This is everyone I know and love and trust!" But the beggar was already a lost shadow in the vast cover of the night.

They walked home together, hand in hand, beginning to tremble now with the awe that follows sudden joy. Kali and Candolel, reluctant to be enclosed again by walls, stood before the hut. Not knowing what else to do, they waited. Holding Kali's head against her shoulder, Abra whispered to her, "Do you remember anything? About being . . . ?"

Kali shook her head, trying to clear it of confusion. "I cannot remember," she said at last. "It was not painful, but it was extremely dark and sad. There were others, and we were all waiting."

"Waiting for what?"

"I'm not sure. I think we were waiting for someone with power."

"Perhaps it was the beggar."

"If it was, where are the rest who were with us? I do not know who they were, but I could feel them and hear them. I think I would know them again if they drew near."

The three waited then in warm silence and wonder until the beggar appeared again, trailing a magnificent white horse behind him. "He has been cared for," explained the beggar, "but his harness and trappings are gone."

"A small loss," said Candolel quietly, caressing his horse's nose. "They can be replaced."

"He is a fast horse, and strong," noted the beggar.

"He is. That is why I named him Roadreeler."

"That name will serve. You will one day have need of his swiftness—but that will be many months from now. Tomorrow is your immediate concern. What is your dream in Glory? Wealth and fame?"

No longer sure of the value of his dreams, Candolel nodded mutely.

"You shall have not fame but success," continued Covenant, "and not wealth but resources. Blessings and property will come to you, but not to be hoarded. They shall be used for others. Glory is indeed a chosen place; your hope is there, as is your destiny. You shall all go. I will follow after you, and then you will follow me." Nodding at Candolel, he said, "You have a house, and a place for business." It was not a question.

"I have a shop for dealing," said Candolel, "and rooms above it. It is small, but it is enough for the three of us."

"It will seem smaller," Covenant smiled. "You will not be three alone for long. I will send others after you, and you must house them until I arrive. They will know your house by this." He handed Candolel a carved slab of wood, weathered well by the wind. "This is my mark. You shall fasten it beside your door."

Candolel took it and turned it over in his hands. "Are you not coming with us?"

"No," Covenant replied. "I have other places to visit—other towns."

"Are you needed there?"

"I am, though they do not yet know it. But I am not finished here. I have new names for you all—and new tasks as well." He pointed to Candolel and Kali. "The villagers think the two of you are dead and lying beneath the trees. Let them believe it as long as they will; let your names die here as well. You should carry new names into your new life.

"Instead of Candolel, let us bring forth a new Candle—a great candle to shine for the Elder God—and Moonflower, the maiden, to bloom beside him and help fuel his fire."

He turned to Abra. "And you they will not miss, though your life is not yet ended. The tales you have been told so faithfully will not stop with you; I promise you many children to sit at your feet and listen to you. Now your name shall be Trueteller."

Candle looked uncomfortably at Covenant, not understanding his need for a new name.

"It is a small thing I ask of you," said Covenant gently. "Were it not for me, and for the faith of this woman in the stories of old, you would be sleeping tonight—and every night forever—in the embrace of the earth."

He turned to Abra—Trueteller—again. "Some other wanderer will come and sleep in this place and call it home, even as you did."

"How did you know that? I have not told you that tale."

"Perhaps it is time you did. You have not yet told me all your griefs."

"Please," she asked of him, "please, before you send us away—I have a pilgrimage to make."

"I know," he answered, drawing her aside from the others. "There is one whom you have not spoken of, one who is neither here nor buried here."

"My husband."

"Where is he?"

"Gone. Perhaps dead . . . if not dead, then long vanished. He left me here many years ago. We lived alone in the forests to the south of here. I was already with child"—she gestured to her daughter—"when he left to sell the good things he gathered from the floor of the forest. He did not return that day, that week, the next, or even after the next moon."

"And you came here?"

"I had to. My time was drawing near, and I had no one. There were wolves in the deep woods and lions in the hills, even as there are now. Kali and I have stayed on the edge of this unfriendly village, but each year I have returned to the house in the wilderness and made my mark again beside the door, trusting that if he ever returns he will know that I am still alive. The arrow I have carved there points north; if he returns, he will know where to look for me."

"My path leads south from here, through those very forests. I will make this year's mark for you," offered Covenant. "I will carve the sign of Glory beneath it, and I will make my mark under that as well. Should he ever come that way again, perhaps he will know that I have been here as well."

Then the beggar spoke to them all, and they listened, and when they were done they began to pack their few possessions into a crude saddlebag.

Moonflower stopped suddenly and turned to Candle. "I cannot find your pledge necklace," she said nervously. "My mother kept it when I died, but now it is no longer on the mantle."

"Nor can I find yours," he answered sadly. "It may have been taken from me after . . . after the fight in the square." Disappointment betrayed itself in their eyes.

"What have you lost, children?" asked the beggar. Moonflower thought he sounded more patient than curious, as though he already knew the answer and were playing a child's game.

"Candle gave me a pledge on a chain for my neck," she answered, "half a medallion that had our names intertwined. His half—the part he kept—completes my half, makes it whole. Now both pieces are gone."

"Your pledge to each other is more than hammered metal," said Covenant. "Your promises may endure even when silver ornaments are lost, though a word is easily broken and the metal cannot be rendered without tools." He smiled. "You will find this to be true for many things: that which is the most fragile is also the most durable. And those things you think most durable will be the first to perish. I say to you that the sea will burn up and the mountains fall before your pledges fail."

They contented themselves with that promise. And as the morning brought them sufficient light, the three rode away bareback on Roadreeler. They traveled east and then north in a long curve that would bring them at last to Glory.

The beggar, with a sack of food for himself, started off toward the south on Trueteller's donkey, the forests far ahead and the great hills rolling in their midst. He stroked the donkey's flank as they paced along. "You should bear a better name as well, my friend. Let us call you Kingsburro, for someday you shall carry on your shoulders the King of Glory."

The people of the village, still watching the northern road for a sign of the healer, took no notice of any of them.

THREE

The Lion
of the
Hills

THE FINAL TINGES OF THE DAY HAD JUST FADED FROM THE
forest. Unseen in the underbrush, a thin young man watched
as his sister placed her newborn infant on the rock slab in the
wilderness. A lion roared somewhere—not very far away—
and the girl vanished quickly along the narrow path through
the trees. The lad waited only a heartbeat, and then he
bounded to the rock across the clearing and snatched the baby
girl, still sleeping from the drugged milk.

And then the moonshadow of the lion fell over them, and
its roar ruled the darkness.

Screaming defiance, Damon lashed out with his dagger
while shielding the baby between his back and the stone. Still
cloaked in darkness, the lion roared in his face and slapped his
blade spinning into the curtained reaches of the forest. Damon

closed his eyes and waited for the end.

Lions smell like sudden death and savaged meat and terror, he thought, surprised, *but not this one.*

Then the roaring stopped, leaving only his heart thundering in his chest and his gasps rending the night. Damon opened his eyes—and blinked, for there was no lion, only a man outlined in the moonlight. It was a beggar, wrapped in a dusty cloak and brandishing a staff. The beggar lowered his stick and said, "You will not need your weapon. There is no harm for her here—or for you either, this night of all nights."

Damon could think of nothing to say or do. Clinging to the child, he slumped down and backward against the side of the rock.

The beggar smiled at his silence and sat down on a fallen tree trunk to wait. Though the day had been warm, the evening was already fierce with cold, and their breath left halos around their heads.

"Where did the lion go?" gasped Damon at last.

"There was no lion," the beggar said. "There is only me. I mean no harm to your sister's child, or to the man Damon who guards her."

"How do you know who we are?" Damon asked, suspicion scraping rough edges into his voice.

"I know many things that are not readily visible," replied the beggar. "I know not only your names, but why you are here."

"But this child has no name!" said Damon. "Her christening was to be called *unwanted,* and to be cast away for the lions to devour."

"You are wrong almost beyond measure," replied the beggar, gazing away into the forested darkness at some sound only he had heard. "She has a lovely name indeed, but no one has bothered to give it to her yet. That, in part, is why I came."

"Who are you?"

"My name is Covenant, and I am true to my name."

"What sort of riddles are you speaking?" Damon looked

27

around uneasily. "I should be gone by now. There are lions about."

"My name is Covenant, and I am true to my name. There is nothing for you to fear tonight. I am the lord of all lions, and I send them where I will. They will stay away until we have finished here."

"What do you mean? I have done what I came to do."

"And what will you do now?" the beggar asked, leaning toward Damon and his burden. "She has no one to turn to and nowhere to go. You have cast your lot with her, and now you also have no one to turn to and nowhere to go. You came to rescue her, and you did so at great risk."

"I had my knife."

"And you tried to use it. Had a true lion come against you instead of this old beggar, I know you would not have been less brave. You would not, however, still be alive."

The beggar settled back against the tree again as he spoke. "Even as you have saved her from perishing, so have I saved you both. And now I would deliver both of you into a different life.

"You must carry this child to Glory," continued Covenant, "and see how I deal with the unwanted of the world, for this child is not alone." He turned and faced the great rock, his arms spread in a mixture of appeal and agony. "There are many wretched rocks akin to this in lonely places, where the young and unwanted or the old and unneeded are left to perish—either from the teeth of the cold or the teeth of the lion."

"But where is the lion?" Damon asked, still nervously scanning the darkness.

The beggar growled low but surprisingly loud in the stillness, and there was no longer any doubt from whose throat the roar had issued. Damon scrambled backward, clutching the child and trying to cradle her at the same time.

"You need not be afraid," said the beggar calmly. "Although everything evil in the woods is terrible, not everything terrible in the woods is evil. And a fierce outcry is essential; if I did not come and split the night with the song of the mighty, the exposers would linger to make sure their outcasts died. This way they run, and believe, and are secure in their folly." He lowered his voice, and his eyes bored through the darkness. "But you must answer this question: Will you leave your family for me? And for her? I offer you both a home in Glory."

A donkey brayed twice in the near distance while Damon thought.

"I cannot go back," he said, "and I cannot go with you. My mother is dead, and my father is old and ill. I am sure that my sister will also bring him to this rock when he is too feeble to stop her. How can I rescue him from the lion as well? I cannot hide in these hills to wait for my father. But I cannot return home either."

"I know your father well enough, though he does not yet know me. I will know the season and the hour of his trial in the wilderness, and I will send you to aid him. That is my promise to you. But if you will receive my promises, you must obey my commands: Go to Glory, and take the girl with you."

"But what of my sister?" Damon asked. "She may turn and do this again."

"She will not," he said, and turned the question around. "But what of your sister? Why did she cast this one aside?"

"She would be happy only with a boy."

"Then she must wait in vain. I have spoken a word against her, and she shall bear no son, and never a child again. She will long for her boy forever and he will not come, because she has despised the child that was given her."

Damon had no reply, and he gazed past the beggar into the dark distance. The girl in his arms slept on.

"Except for my father, there is little to leave," Damon replied after a measured pause. "My sister does not honor me, and her husband has no respect for me. I have no children, for no woman would have me." He turned his face toward the silhouette of the beggar. Old swellings and wounds beneath scars showed plainly in the moonlight. "I know that no one wants me, and I can think of none who need me—save for this one who scarcely knows that I am here, and does not understand anything at all."

"She needed you, and you came. You needed me, and I came as well."

"I do not understand," he said, puzzled.

"You have no more need to understand than she does. You can only reach out and take what is given to you."

"But why did you come tonight?" asked Damon. "Surely you cannot come here every night!"

"I do not need to journey here every night, for most nights there is nothing here that a lion would want. It is my business to be wherever and whenever I am needed. I knew she would be here. And it pleased me that you would be here as well."

The unseen donkey brayed again. The baby roused and began to cry. Damon could not comfort her, but she ceased her howling when the beggar eased her onto his shoulder and murmured to her.

"Come," said the beggar, "there is a house nearby. Let us go in from the frost of the night." He turned and walked away with the baby.

"A house? There is nothing in this wilderness but the dens of animals!"

"Now, perhaps, but once there was a family here. Their dwelling still stands."

He led Damon into the underbrush, pausing once to point wordlessly to the ground at their feet. Damon scrabbled in the soft loam and recovered his knife. He slipped it back into his belt without comment, and they moved deeper into the forest. Soon they came to a stand of trees where a donkey browsed the remains of a scattered sack of grain. Beyond those trees was an abandoned cottage, its walls hidden by years of vines, the wooden door long since rotted and fallen in.

Damon could hardly see at all, but the beggar seemed to know the way. Once through the arch of the doorway, Damon could see the tiny fire glowing in the heap of stones that had once been the fireplace. For the first time, there was enough light for him to see the beggar's face clearly.

He was not handsome, but his visage inspired trust. He was neither ancient nor fresh-faced, and both warm and worn at the same time. The beggar returned the baby to Damon and stepped outside again to throw down more grain for the donkey. The child remained content and fell asleep in Damon's arms.

Damon looked about him carefully, though there was little enough left in the cottage. On the post that had once held the door, he found the mark of a heart carved large upon the wood. There was an arrow emblazoned beneath it, and many marks below that. All these marks were gray with time, and he could not quite number them in the ruddy, shifting light. Sixteen? Seventeen? It was hard to tell. There were three new chiseled signs at the bottom and a handful of fresh wood shavings on the floor.

The beggar joined him at the doorway and asked, "Do you see this mark?" His fingers lingered on the weathered heart.

"Yes."

"It is the evidence of old love never abandoned, still proclaimed for all the world to see. Do you see these many notches below it?"

Damon nodded.

"These are the signs of hope long nurtured against fear in the face of the witness of time—one mark for each lonely year that has passed. Such a love is not easily defeated. Do you see this new notch?"

"I see it."

"I put it there with my own hands early this evening. It is the mark for this year. And do you know the symbol beneath that?"

31

"All know that sign. It is the mark of Glory."

The beggar nodded. "And beneath that?"

"I do not know that sign."

"It is my mark, and this same sign is emblazoned on a house in Glory. Find it, and tell the people there you have come in my name."

"But they will not know my name."

"They will welcome you anyway. And your name, from now on, shall be Lionheart. Old names are good, new ones better, and true ones best of all. It is a name you should bear for the moment, for you dared to face the lion for one who had no other champion. It is also a name you should bear for the future, for I call you to take my place in rescuing others from the rocks of exposure. You shall lose nothing and gain much. I promise you that if you leave your family here behind, you will have both children and parents of your own forever."

Damon gazed down at the baby. "I already have her, to begin with."

"You could not keep her for long, by yourself."

"Why not?" the boy bristled.

"You have cared for children before, but never for the newborn. She would die in the midst of all the love you would pour out upon her. But," the beggar continued, "her future is secure in me. It is your future that must be attended to."

"I do not know that I can trust you."

"You can trust no one else. You have no more choices, it seems. The child trusts me, though she chooses for reasons you have long forgotten. I tell you, go to Glory and see for yourself. The house of Candle will host you until another place is made ready. Ask after Trueteller there, to help you care for the child. Soon, I will be there as well." He leaned over and produced a small sack from the shadows behind him. "Here. You must find the way from here, for I have other business to see to. But I shall not send you alone to Glory. The road is long, and it wanders, and there are animals that threaten. Therefore, I will call to you two friends you need fear no longer."

He growled softly into the night, two separate calls, and was answered in kind. A great shadow appeared from the shadows, and another behind it. Two massive lions emerged from the doorway into the dim circle of the fire, and Damon knew there was no place to run.

"Do not be afraid, Lionheart," said the beggar. "You dared the lions for her, and for your bravery you shall have them to command. There are other wild beasts than lions, but none of them will bother you as long as you are escorted. Wolves will not come near you. Nor will bears disturb your passing, and snakes will slither away at the sound of your approach. These two will carry you to the edge of Glory."

"Carry?"

"You will ride." He beckoned to the larger lion—a male, Damon could see now. The lion came to Covenant and crouched at his feet. Covenant mounted and drew Damon up in front of him before the boy realized what was happening.

"My beast waits in the trees over there," the beggar continued. "Our road is long, and we have not yet come to the end of it." Then Covenant dismounted and left Damon on the lion's back. "The bag holds food and water for your journey. Sit lightly, and twist one fist into his mane, and you will go where he goes. As for her," he said, pointing to the infant cradled in Damon's free arm, "she will sleep much, and she has been provided for." Damon looked bewildered. "You will recognize the provision when her hunger comes." The second shadow, a lioness, nudged his leg, and he began to understand.

Damon's decision crystallized within him, and he knew that he need not give voice to it. The bulk of the great beast beneath him brought him peace now, surprisingly. He stretched and could almost hear the beggar smiling in the darkness. "I will go," he said. "But surely *she* cannot continue without a name."

"Then let us call her Woodswaif. I know her true name, her final name, but for now that shall be my secret alone. Do you know enough now to begin?"

"I think so," replied Lionheart, watching the lioness drift to nuzzle her mate. "But how can I return later and take your place? I am not a lion."

"Neither am I—as you can see," returned the beggar, spreading his arms again, his smile beaming brighter than the moonlight outside. "But one need not be a lion to be their king. And I can teach you how to roar."

——— FOUR ———

After
the
Rain

T HE BEGGAR ON THE DONKEY RODE SLOWLY BETWEEN THE vast fields of grain, past the open pit strewn with small stones, and through the waiting gate into the village. Storm clouds gathered like gray mountains in the distance, several hours' riding away. The village was quiet—far too quiet for midday. The beggar heard only one faint sound, a low rumbling from the far side of the open square that marked the village center. He dismounted and led his beast through the squat stone buildings toward the murmur.

The square was empty, save for a stone altar, a tall iron stake, and a small dirty building of weathered rock that leaned away from the sun. The altar was covered with road dust and old chaff, except where a few stalks of grain had been placed. The beggar tested them and found them fresh, as though they had lain there only a night. The stake stood behind the altar—tall, stark, charred, with old ashes circling the metal spike. And the building, only a few paces wide and long, bore iron bars in the few tiny windows.

The beggar moved on beyond the square. There, between two of the buildings, an old man huddled over a wooden framework, grinding grain. His eyes were closed, dark and sunken in their sockets, and his cheeks were hollow. The beggar could hear now a monotonous cough, a ceaseless rattle that drove quavers through the old man's gaunt frame, already rocking with the rumbling rhythm of the stone wheel.

The beggar paused in the shadows and watched until the grinder, aroused by some slight sound, opened his eyes and saw him. He loosed the handle of the wheel and the sound of the rolling stones died away.

"Ho, stranger." He focused first on the beggar, and then peered at the sky, as if seeing it for the first time in many hours. "You bring the rain with you."

"Aye. And you should bless me for it. All your fields are dry."

"Let them wither. They only bring me burdens I cannot bear. The grain comes here, and I must grind it."

"You grind alone?"

"I grind alone because I grind slowly." He paused to hack in the dust. "The wagons bring the grain in the evenings. We—the old ones—grind all night and sleep by day if we can. This is the spring harvest, and all the able are working in the fields." He waved a gnarled hand over the many sacks of whole grain stacked beside his stone. "This is left of my share from last twilight. I have turned the wheel all night and all day."

"And if you do not finish?"

"For those who can no longer work—or will not—the pit of stones is waiting." The old man shuddered as he reached to resume his task. "I bid you welcome, for myself, but I also give

you warning. If you have the strength, you would do well to pass on. This village holds no love for beggars, and it makes no room for hungry idle mouths."

"I do not beg for meals. But I accept freely, even as I give freely."

"And what do you give so freely?"

"To prove that my mouth is not idle—a story."

"Yes. Tell me a story, if you dare to stand idle. A traveler's tale may bring some ease to this weary old heart." He began to turn the wheel.

"In another village over the hills there was a man . . ." His words hummed soft and slow and soothing like buzzing bees in the warm, close afternoon.

The old man slept over his wheel, and the rolling stones rolled slowly into stillness.

When the old man started awake, he saw the sun lying far beyond the noon zenith. He grabbed frantically for the wheel, but he stopped when he saw the sacks of ground grain stacked neatly beside the framework and his own work bins now empty. The beggar had not moved.

The two men stared at each other while storm clouds grumbled in the corners of the darkening sky.

"I know who you are now," the old man said softly. "There were rumors of you, but not many believed. Unlike some who are not old enough to be wise, I have heeded what I have heard."

"And you believe now because all your grain is ground?"

"No mortal could grind all that in a mere span of hours. And I know you did not turn this wheel."

"You do well to believe, but you believe on shallow deeds. The grinding of grain is a small thing."

"In your eyes, perhaps, but not in mine. I am grateful for your gift."

"Then share your meal with me. Let us feast together."

"On what? I draw poor rations for grinding. Nothing else

is mine but a tiny room in the shadow of the walls. Little else will come to me. I have no food fit for the gods."

"Then let us eat this." The beggar rose and slung a sack of the fresh-ground meal over his patient donkey's back. "It will feed the three of us handsomely."

"It is not allowed!" the old man protested. "All the grain belongs to the village, until the elders hand it to those who need it."

"And do we not need it?" the beggar continued, fastening the sack in place with bits of old rope. "Is there no provision for wayfarers? Or for the hands that ground it? Even the workers eat the fruit of the orchard as it passes through their hands. And the oxen that pull the threshing sledge may browse the ground when the sledge is still. Come. We deserve this meal. Let us prepare a supper fit for the weary."

The old man and the beggar sat in the shelter of the tiny room. The graincakes were soon gone, slaying hunger in their passing.

"Soon," the old man said, "soon the wagons will come and I must grind again."

"They give you no rest."

"No. The greedy never rest. And neither may the poor."

"And the law of the elders?"

"Their law has freed the village from the burden of caring for those who cannot contribute. The aged, the infirm, the diseased—they are taken out to be stoned. It is what they shall do to me when I can no longer turn the wheel. Each night the task grows longer, and I weaker." He gazed at the doorway and wept inside his heart where he thought no one could hear. "I hear the wagons now."

"No. That is only the thunder that heralds the rain—and the rain will come before the wagons. But the storm is not yet upon us, and even the sun gives us a few hours. Do not the workers gather until it is too dark to see?"

"They come home at dusk." The two men watched the shadows lengthen across the doorway.

"You have heard tales of me," the beggar said. "And you believe. Yet you have asked nothing of me. Is your fear so great?"

"I have fear, yes. And also poverty. I am so poor that you have nothing to offer me."

"I gave you a story to warm your heart and rest your body. And now your heart cries out to me across the room. Name its need and I will fill you."

The old man wept openly. "I know of you. You bring life to the dead, and grain to the hungry, and wine to the thirsty, and strength to the faint . . . I desire none of those things."

"Have you no love dead and buried? No hunger? No thirst? No weakness? I cannot accept that you are a man without need."

"I have my needs. But it may happen that a man—especially an old man—may no longer desire to have his needs fulfilled." He stood slowly and led the beggar to the doorway, where they could see through the village, over the far wall and beyond to a river, with trees rooted deep into the banks. "I have my needs. I am always hungry. I thirst. I am weary of my weakness and even of my weariness itself. And I have my beloved dead." He pointed to the trees by the river. "I buried her beneath the willows," he continued softly, "and now she waits for me in the City beyond the rainbow."

"The rainbow?"

"We used to walk there beneath the trees by the water, where the sun sets like fire and diamonds over the mountains. When the rain comes in the evenings, the sun leaves a rainbow behind as its final shadow. Under the rainbow are those mountains, and those mountains are the end of the world."

"And beyond them? Nothing?"

"Beyond them must be the true West, where the City lies and the Elder God dwells. We promised to wait for one another there. One night, after the rain, while we wondered at the rainbow from this riverbank, she died."

"Has your grief passed?"

"My grief was small, and not for her, because I saw the peace of her passing. With my own eyes I saw the smile that came as the last pain was fading. She opened her eyes then, and they were filled with marvels as she gazed into a wondrous land I could not see. My grief for me was swallowed by my joy for her. I buried her there between the roots of the giant willow, our private place of rainbows. Even now, when the rains come and go, I may stand in my doorway and see the bright colors arching over her grave."

The beggar stepped down from the doorway. "I should be honored if you would walk with me there."

When they reached the riverbank, the old man broke the silence. "Why are you here in this town? One who comes here can only be coming here. There is only the one road. To the west are only the mountains, and on either side only our fertile fields. No roads point eastward save the paths of the great grain wagons.

"And you wake legends with your footsteps. It is said that strangers who come before the rain bring with them darkness and death."

"So I have heard. But is it not also said that a stranger who lingers after the rain brings a blessing?"

"So some say. But only if there is a rainbow."

The beggar traced circles in the grass with his foot. "Not all the old legends are true. And some are truer than you might imagine." He looked up suddenly at the old man. "And you, in your turn, are a strange man. You know who I am, yet you ask nothing."

"I know what you would have me ask, and I will not. *She* is the pain closest to my heart, yet I would not call her back to me. Some deeds are better left undone. What joy could she return to? The grainwheel awaits her, to drain her and steal her strength again, as it does daily to me. They would soon take her out to be stoned. No. Please do not impose such a kindness upon us."

They watched the ripples in the river.

"I hear the wagons," the old man said. "Or do you say it is only the thunder?"

"No. The wagons come. But you need not return to meet them. There is still time for you to seek a gift."

"I am grateful to you, but I desire nothing more."

"No secret dreams? No untold wishes?"

"Only . . . only one." He scarcely dared breathe the words. "Perhaps you are the only one who might understand." He gazed unseeingly at the mountains. "I dream often of dying here, here beneath this tree where she lies—of dying peacefully, and not under the hurling weight of many stones or in the heat of the hungry flames—of dying with her face in my heart and her name on my lips. But I would need gentle hands to bury me beside her, and I have no man to lower me into the embrace of the earth."

The beggar's next words hung like sunbeams in the air. "Many have sought a good life and more of it. You may choose a way which is better yet."

The old man let silence preface his words.

"Before I was yet this old," he began, "before this village grew complete in its corruption and enslavement by love of gold and grain, one day in seven was a day of rest—born from the word of the Elder God, I know, but by then little more than a tradition.

"On such days I would wake, weary, fearful, not remembering at first that no work would be required of me that day. And then it would burst upon me like lightning that more rest awaited me, that a prolonging of sleep was mine for the taking. And how often I longed to hold that glorious lightning in my hand and make it a lasting joy—to wake and find an eternity of unbroken rest at hand." He opened his arms wide to the mountains and the hidden lands beyond. "I believe that was what sparked her last and most lasting smile—the beckoning, the rest, the peace, the waking in the west that makes all that has gone before a long and troubled sleeping." He dropped his arms and faced the beggar. "Is such a gift within your power?"

"It is. The one who gives forth may also withdraw his hand. Only the ones who are bold of heart may claim them both as equal blessings. I speak for him, for I am he. Ask what you will."

"I have seen the first blessing. It is the second that I ask from your hand."

"Then behold your rest! It comes for you with loving hands. Because you asked me not for small favors that perish, I give you the everlasting desire of your heart." Wooden wheels rumbled along the dirt roads behind them. "And you need not go to meet the wagons."

"If . . . If I may . . . I should like to enjoy this last rain, and see one final rainbow."

The beggar laughed, and the old man's unbidden tears shared that burst of joy. "By all means! Let there be soft rains and the light that arches over! And then, after the rain, I shall give you rest."

He waved his arms across the swollen sky, and beneath a new prismed curve of color the rain came to them over the fields like lambs running.

FIVE

Trial
by
Fire

Y OU WILL STAND TRIAL TOMORROW FOR THE SLAYING OF the old man!" The young man jeered through the bars at the beggar in the tiny stone cell. "But the verdict is sure. More than one of us saw you bury him."

Grain wagons rolled through the streets outside, bearing home a double load of harvest and weary people. The beggar, eyeing the jailer as though they sat at table for supper and were not separated by iron bars, spoke at last. "There is much that you did not see. And much more that you do not."

"What is that to me? *You* are the one who will pay the price. Do you deny the old man's death?"

"I do not. But you do wrong to call it murder."

"Let the flames decide your innocence. You will have your trial by fire. And just it is, too, although I myself would chain you to the wheel and let you grind your life away. Or cast you into a pit and test your flesh with stones. There are others of the same mind as well. You anger many when you hinder the harvest."

"If all in this village work, how do you justify yourself? You are too lame to work in the fields."

Anger flushed the young man's face as he forced himself to his full height. "My leg is not too twisted to drive a wagon! Besides, this town would be poorer without me. I entertain them at night when their work is done. I am their balladeer, their poet, their historian, their jester, their teller of tales— and their law-binder and jailer when someone breaks the laws of the elders.

"I am Barid, and my brothers own the finest land here. I am not a man to be dismissed lightly!" He turned away from the bars and hobbled across the square to join a small, gathering crowd.

The beggar could see half the square from his window. There was a high metal stake set in the center, a few paces from the altar of the Elder God. Down a side street he could see the wheel that the old man had so wearily turned.

He watched the wagons passing, and noted the few who paused to throw a sheaf of grain down onto the basin of the altar. Barid's voice carried clearly to him, soaring and swooping, singing a rude and bawdy ballad to the cheers of sweaty men slaking their thirst with mugs of fermented grain. Barid possessed a fine voice, and the beggar reflected long upon him.

Later, Barid's face appeared at the cell's window. "Beggar! We would try you tonight, but the Harvest Feast is almost upon us, and we are weary, and there is much to be made ready. Perhaps tomorrow, as entertainment."

"Barid?"

Only a grunt came in answer.

"Do you not know other songs?" the beggar asked. "Any songs that do not dishonor the gifts the Elder God gave to men?"

Barid laughed through the barred opening. "The Elder God! I suppose you're one of those fools who would throw good grain to waste upon the altar!" The hardness in his eyes softened, and his voice gained a faint tinge of sadness. "I need no other songs, only new ones like those I sang tonight. They throw me coppers now, and sometimes silver for the choicer stories. There would be no payment for a sentimental ballad."

"Is it in your memory or your lore why you feast tomorrow?"

"For the grain, of course! The flood gates of our life have opened wide, and golden is the tide! Why should we not celebrate?"

"You do not remember why the Harvest Feast was first held? Or when? By whose command? Do you recall a time before there was grain here?"

"No. We have always held the feast. And the grain has ever been here. Go to sleep, old man, and enjoy it. You may not have many more wakenings."

The beggar spoke to the darkness where Barid had been. "You do not know these things? Your fathers did. And I shall remind you tomorrow." His eyes overflowed with sadness as he leaned back on the prisoner's bench. Barid returned later, full of spirits and mirth, and collapsed into sleep in the dust outside the cell.

*   *   *

The next evening Barid brought the prisoner to the center of the square and set him before the people. He read aloud the charges and turned to the beggar.

"The assembly has met and has decided. We do not know if you slew the old man. We do know that you buried him by the river. Therefore our judgment is this: you shall stand trial by fire. Here at this stake we shall bind you and kindle the flames. If you perish, you are deemed guilty, and justice will have been done. If you endure, you are innocent of the man's death.

"But if innocent, you will take his place at the wheel until the harvest is finished. We cannot afford the loss of a laborer." Turning to the people, he commanded them, "Take him to the fire."

They bound him there, and brought wood and kindling and oil.

But they could not light the fire.

The kindling dripped with oil, but the sparks sputtered out as though the brands had been thrust into water. The fire-striker muttered and moved away from the stake.

Then the beggar raised his hands and the bonds fell away. He leaped to the top of the altar. "Your fire is not enough!" He pointed his finger at the stake and the fuel flared in a single monstrous tongue of flame, driving the watchers back with its heat. The wood was consumed in a blink of bright fury. In a moment only the twisted iron of the stake showed above the smoldering ashes.

The smoke scattered on the breeze as the beggar turned to the cringing crowd. "You have brought judgment down on your own heads. Had you condemned me for what you supposed to be the slaying of a man, a free and worthy being, I would merely have walked away from you. But you have tried me for the destruction of that which you viewed as your own property—a nameless slave whom you yourself would have killed in sickness, a possession useful to you only in your service to your god. *Your* god, and not the God of your fathers."

He stared at them all, his eyes daring them to move. No one left, and he continued in a lower but even stronger voice. "I stand on this altar to the Elder God. Do you worship him?" He brandished a fistful of offered grain. "Some of you do. I hold your offerings and firstfruits, and I know your hearts and see your faithfulness. I know you sing songs of praise and thanks to the True God, to the One who ordained this feast and granted you this harvest." Then he named their names, one by one, and their hearts were strangely and suddenly

lifted as he called them to stand by the altar at his right hand. Slowly and cautiously, the called ones eased their way through the crowd and obeyed.

"I bless you for your faithfulness," the bold beggar said to those who had moved at his bidding. "Yet I have this against you: You saw injustice, greed, and the growing idols in the fields, but you said nothing and did not raise your voice in protest. Behold! You must share the ordeal of the others. But know that I will strengthen your hearts, and it will surely pass."

He turned to the small multitude of the ones who still stood on his left. "As for the rest of you, you have forgotten the faith of your fathers and unlearned their gratitude. This altar was built by zealous men in a barren land—men who prayed to the Elder God and waited patiently. Seven times they prayed, for seven days, and on the seventh day the Elder God turned their wasteland into fertile fields. This altar was here, built by their hands, before there was grain here. When the firstfruits were reaped, they were offered here. And on that day they declared a Harvest Feast to be held each year, that the kindness of the Elder God might not be forgotten.

"But you have forgotten. You remember not the Elder God but the false golden god who grows in your fields. Do you doubt me? Then look to the pain of your hearts as your god is put to the test of fire. For it is not I who stands here for judgment, but you and your chosen god!"

The sheaves of grain flared suddenly in his hands. "Behold the acceptable sacrifice! Behold the pleasing smoke!" A pillar of fire rose from the altar, wrapping the beggar in flames, yet not consuming him. The burning reached high into the sky and dark rolling clouds gathered around the pillar, spreading out over all the heavens. Thunder rolled overhead and on every side, smothering the screams that came unbidden to the throats of the watchers.

"Behold the judgment—and the death of your golden god!"

From the heart of the cloud, vast lightnings streaked the sky, striking again and again around them, forking the fields with flame. Fire raged through the standing grain too quickly to follow, consuming barns of stored grain in single deep explosions. The earth trembled. Where the fire had passed, the earth smoked.

Huddled together, the stunned villagers watched through their fingers, afraid to cry out, afraid to run, afraid to breathe. Then the lightning ceased and the clouds swirled backward into the standing pillar. Then the pillar collapsed with slow violence, leaving the beggar standing alone upon the altar.

"A trial by fire. And the verdict? Where is your god now to proclaim his innocence?

"And your own innocence? You grieve the smoldering earth." Only a few scattered stands of grain now stood unmarked. "Even the soil is lifeless. It has returned to the wasteland from which it came. Your god has abandoned you in his death, and with him goes your life as well."

He turned to Barid. "Approach the altar. I have not yet finished with you." Barid, afraid to obey, too frightened not to obey, crawled awkwardly to the foot of the altar.

The villagers trembled. The beggar dismissed the ones on his left hand, saying, "Go to your homes. You have not honored the Elder God, and he will not honor you until you repent of your hardness of heart. Never again shall this land bear fruit for you. Go, and make plans to journey on from this place."

Then he dismissed the few on his right hand, laying a blessing upon their heads as they went. When the square was once more empty, he turned at last to Barid, sprawled in the dust beneath the altar. "You have not honored me, but you shall. Stay here with the faithful, for mercy follows judgment, and I have not finished my work here."

During the next two days, wagons thundered slowly through the town, carrying not grain but households and goods and people away to the towns to the east. The old man's wheel sat unneeded and unheeded in the middle of the emptying village.

Only a few remained with the beggar to watch the exodus. And when the dust had settled behind the last wagon, they began to speak with him.

"We have done as you said. We bought all their fields. But why? Why did you bid us trade our last silver and remaining gold for worthless soil? And why were our fields not consumed? Forgive our boldness, but you have given us only commands and no answers."

The beggar gazed out over the scorched fields. "Yours is the right now to ask questions, because you have already obeyed. Your own fields were not burned because you had already offered your firstfruits. Your firstfruits ransomed the rest of your crops—that which was in the fields and that which is now laid in your barns.

"The others hated you. Why should they not sell you the land that would never yield for them again? They are not fools to pass by profit. Your gold and silver are honored in all the land—but even their soil was burned. And you have bought it now. By deed of law?"

"Yes."

"Witnessed by the elders?"

"Yes."

"Can anyone argue that you forced their lands from them?"

"No."

"Then the land is yours forever. No blessings remain for them. But the land will yet bless you when I return and bless the land."

"But what shall we do now?"

"Abide here. You have sufficient grain to survive here until the winter. There is none left to sell, but you have no pressing need either for money or for the things that money can buy.

"Await my return. I shall surely come before winter. Wait

for me. Wait with the same faith that has been your salvation so far. If any among you should lose courage and set out toward the towns and fields of the east, let the rest of you buy their land honestly from them.

"As for the land, let it savor its rest now. Greed has abused it, and only now shall it have peace."

Then Barid spoke. "And what of me? Shall I, too, wait? I own no land, I have no inheritance. It was only at your command that I did not board the wagons with my brothers. Shall I starve here?" he asked bitterly.

The beggar took the man's elbow in his hand and urged him away from the square. "It would not be an evil yoke for you to learn humility. The rest would feed you—but not for your twisted songs and tales. Indeed, I do not think you have the heart to sing such now. They would feed you in love for you and obedience to me, and that would shatter your pride.

"But I choose another way to break you, bind you, make you whole and set you free. Come with me." And they wandered toward one of the houses lying between the square and the willowed river. The beggar stood before the door and said, "You are one who wields power, yet you will not yield readily to my power. I know this, for I know all men. Enter this house with me, and see for yourself that high power need not always be terrible." They entered, and a child met them—a child with tears in her eyes, a child who stared with hope at the beggar.

Barid asked in low tones, "Does she cry for the loss of the grain?"

"No. She is too young to understand. But she is old enough to know other pains, pains that are larger to her than ruined fields." He bent down and spoke softly to her. She disappeared into the depths of the house. When she returned, she carried something in her arms.

"Behold the source of her tears." The beggar reached out and gently plucked from her arms a kitten. "The wagons, leaving, left more than simply tracks in the dust." Barid saw the mangled legs and the heaving flank and the pain-glazed eyes, and something hot and piercing flamed in his heart. His hand trembled against his own leg, and visions of other wagon wheels in another year danced in his memory.

"Loud words, and rude, are not all that move you," the beggar said, "nor are violence and destruction the only deeds that I do. Behold." He stroked the kitten, and in his hands he made it whole again. It mewed and licked his hand, and he gave it to Barid. "This is the first lesson. Give the child her beloved, and follow me." The child clung to her kitten and to the beggar's legs for a moment, gazing at him with wordless, open gratitude before happily vanishing into another room.

The beggar urged Barid outside and continued. "Are not ten kittens sold for a single coin? And a lame one tossed away? Yet not one of them is struck down where the Elder God does not see. And are you of less value than a kitten?" He led him to the river, where they sat beneath the willows.

"Is it always your business to interfere?" asked Barid.

"Yes, and it is my pleasure as well. I take delight in proving that the universe holds more than people believe—that there are indeed answers, if you choose to look in the proper places and ask the questions correctly.

"It depends on what brings you joy and hope." The beggar gestured to the west. "Look above you at the mountains and below you at the river. I know that these touch you with beauties that do not dwell in the songs you sing. What of the love of a small child for her pet? Or of the woman who walks arm-in-arm with her chosen husband? Why did you not celebrate the love they share rather than the desires of the women who idle near the alehouse?

"You have been given a fine gift, but you profane both it and the giver, and with them yourself. You know many songs to gladden the appetites of men. I have brought you here now to learn songs to gladden their hearts."

The beggar began to sing. And, after the first song, he told

Barid an ancient story, fascinating the man with his weaving hands. When he spoke, he gestured, and such magic was his as to bring life to the words and breath to the images standing behind. Barid expected, watching, to see worlds appear at his command. And then there was another song, and the fresh beauties in the beggar's words broke over Barid like a thunderstorm.

Barid wept, trembling, feeling old inner walls give and quake and crumble, and then walls within walls, both secret and known, until all his defenses lay in ruins. And still the beggar sang on, spinning stories, relentlessly grinding the shattered shards of hardness into powder and fine dust that scattered before the bright breeze of his words. The words carried wisdom so starkly true that his heart leaped, crying Yes! and was ever after changed. And Barid wept for grief for which he had no tears or words or outlet. He begged the beggar to stop and not to stop, for he could no longer bear either the flow of old truths or their cessation.

The beggar came to an end of his tales. He spoke to the weeping Barid long in healing words, mending where he had rent, soothing where he had sliced away, giving balm where his words had wounded.

"You have heard my songs and listened to my refrains. Do you now desire to learn them?"

"Yes."

"One who sings my songs may no longer sing the songs of the world. Do you still choose mine?"

"Yes. If you will give them to me."

"You cannot receive them until you bury your old songs. Bury them here and now, in this place beside the river."

"I do not know how."

"But I do. They will perish with your name. See you the ground where your tears have fallen? Write your name there."

Barid obeyed, inscribing his name in the dampened dirt.

Then the beggar scooped the earth into his hands and molded the moist soil into a tight ball. "Take it, and throw it into the river." Barid obeyed, and they watched it sink, dissolving again to mud on the river bottom.

"You have no name now, and no songs or tales. Prove to yourself that my words are true. Sing me a song from the alehouse."

Barid could think of none. There was only blankness in his mind, blankness overwritten by the words of the beggar.

"You see? I bring other healings beyond the merely physical. And can you tell me your name?"

He could not.

"Your name was Barid, and you belonged to yourself. You are Wordsmith now, and belong to Covenant, because I have need of you to do my work in my name. Come share my spirit, and no longer the spirits of the alehouse. Come keep not prisoners, but free men; write not bawdy ballads, but truest truth. Observe not fallen festivals with your people, but serve a living Feast to my own. I cannot be all places at once, and it is you I select to be with me and do my bidding. What I show you by night you will tell by day. The tales you unravel in secret, you will spin in the middle of the marketplace.

"Of the others, I ask hard things. Of you I ask harder things still. Do not wait. Do not test your faith with the patience of doing nothing. Follow me instead. Do not wait, but follow me. By my power I have forced your obedience—but I have neither your loyalty nor your devotion. That is why I have spoken to you these words of purest truth and unmixed beauty. I speak these things because I am their source and their lifespring. It is because of these things that I ask your loyalty and your devotion, and not because I have power and am to be feared.

"Will you come, Wordsmith?"

"I have not always lived in this tiny, forsaken village. I was born here, and I have returned here, for nowhere have I found that which satisfied me. Here at least I am among my own people. There are finer singers in Glory, and I was only one voice struggling to be heard in the multitude. But here I stand honored and alone."

"I promise you this: Your voice shall be heard by all and heeded by many, if you come and tell my tales for me. You have seen Glory and turned your back upon it willingly?"

"Gladly, even. It is a place of hollow wholeness."

"Then I bid you do a very hard thing," said Covenant. "Return with me to Glory, for it is there that I have established my house."

"I will—but I saw no house grand enough to hold such power. And I never heard your name. Surely you are well known there?"

"I have founded my house, but it is neither finished nor inhabited. I am well known to those who know their need for me, but not famous to all. But why will *you* follow me? Be sure you know clearly in your own mind. I have called you, but it is not written in the stars that you must heed the call."

Wordsmith drew a bottomless breath and stared at the sky that concealed those same stars. "I follow because you have touched me with the truth. I have found it nowhere else." He knew that the answers were already known to Covenant. He knew also that his responses must be uttered anyway.

"Then leave all you have to these faithful ones. Bring nothing with you, and you shall soon possess more than you can carry."

"I have vowed to you, but I do not even know your name."

"I am Covenant," he said. "But he who calls me Covenant must also call me Master. My name is Covenant, for I keep my promises. Even when you do not understand me at all, I will be faithful to you. You have vowed many times to do many things," he continued, "and you have withdrawn your word each time. This time I will hold you to your word. And you shall never regret it, though your own vows return to puzzle you."

"But what are you promising me?"

"My promise is nothing—or everything: nothing you believe you've always wanted, but everything you've always needed." He paused, searching Wordsmith's face. "Have you further questions for me now? If not, then we shall leave in the morning."

But Wordsmith lingered to talk, and their words that night outlasted the shadows and outshone the stars.

———— SIX ————

Trial
Without
Fire

THE WARMTH OF THE COMPANY SHORTENED THE LONG road to Glory.

The two men spoke now and again, but there were long silences that neither chose to break. After their initial night of challenge and long talk, even gestures were enough to convey volumes. And Wordsmith learned from Covenant even in the silence. Covenant smiled and pointed much, moving his hands to underline the truth that had already been uttered. Wordsmith saw and understood. He thought much and wondered at the things that had happened to him in only a handful of days.

Wordsmith was weary, and he wondered if Covenant was tired as well. The beggar walked like an aged man with sore feet, but he did not speak of his pain or complain against the rough dirt of the road.

The donkey could not carry them both, so they walked and trailed the small beast behind them. Covenant seemed to be in no particular hurry, taking time to examine the flowers by the road and enjoy the birds wheeling in the air. Wordsmith too looked at these things, and he began to appreciate many things he had merely seen before.

The first night out, Wordsmith built the fire and curled between the flames and the rocks behind him, while Covenant curled up alone in the unpenetrated shadows away from the fire—alone save for Kingsburro, untethered, nodding, and seemingly unafraid. Wordsmith wished the beggar were sleeping closer to him; somehow he felt safe with Covenant—though he was still mostly mystified by the beggar and his enigmatic but unarguable ways.

He wondered again about wild animals. He had seen nothing large, but he thought the small animals were exceedingly abundant. All day they had flashed across the edges of his vision, appearing at the edges of the trees to peer at the travelers. Now he could sense their comings and goings around the perimeter of the tiny campfire.

In the morning, he awoke after having slept poorly, suffering from the one-sided heat of the fire and the vigilance necessary to keep it burning. Covenant seemed rested and warm. Wordsmith did not understand how the beggar could sleep so soundly and without fear through the hours of darkness.

For Wordsmith, the second day of their journey faded to a timeless wandering, their way becoming as much a goal as their destination. He was often filled with curious wonder, but he could not easily form his questions into words.

The second night passed like the first. Covenant did not suggest a fire, but he allowed Wordsmith to build one for comfort.

But on the third evening, after a third day of tiny marvels, Covenant stopped Wordsmith as he began to gather wood for the night. "We need no fire tonight," said the beggar.

"But the nights are still cold!" objected Wordsmith. "Summer is not yet here."

"The nights are indeed still sharp, and I feel them as keenly as you do. Nevertheless, I ask you to wait. There are other ways to be warmed than by the fire."

"But what of the animals?"

"What of them?"

"Are you not afraid?"

"I have no need to be afraid. You are afraid and do not sleep, while I fear not and sleep well. You should follow my example. You have already obeyed me—now you must learn to trust me as well. Hold back your hand from the wood. Let the sun warm us a final time before it sets. Then let the darkness come."

Wordsmith sat with Covenant and watched the final fingers of day withdraw from the sky. He was cold. He could feel the fear of the night draw closer, but he made no move to spark a flame in the gathered pile of sticks and dead brush.

Covenant stirred, and said, "Now you shall see. Or rather, you shall *not* see. You have obeyed me before from lack of other choice. Your obedience was born of fear—or awe. Now let your obedience be born of trust. Let the fire be, and what will happen then will be a miracle."

"You will show me another miracle?"

"You will see it, but not all of it. You will feel the rest." He said no more than that.

"All right," said Wordsmith at last.

In the twilight, the small animals came first. Foxes, squirrels—together—and rabbits, badgers . . . *were those wolves?* They all came quietly to Covenant, making only snuffling noises. They settled at his feet and on each side of him, nosing his hands for a few moments before settling down watchfully. The drift of animals deepened, and soon the beggar was nearly covered in a fur blanket that had a life of its own. Their small black eyes watched Wordsmith—not fearfully, or with won-

der, but with interest and, perhaps, amusement.

"You see?" asked Covenant. "The animals are not a danger, if you know how to call their names. You have seen. Now you shall feel."

Complete darkness fell, and Wordsmith tuned his senses to the shadows. Even so, he did not see the beasts approaching, and the first he knew of them was the rasp of their claws in his ears and the blast of their breath in his face. He did not—dared not—move. A giant warmth bumped him from one side; a matching bulk pressed against him on the other side and poured its heat into his needy body. A host of smaller, squeaking animals filled in the gaps before him and behind him.

Still trying not to move, Wordsmith fell asleep. He dreamed of bears and lions, but only rabbits and squirrels were left when he awakened. Many pawprints—both great and small—had been scampered in the earth. A blend of heavy, warm scents lingered in the air, and he traced his fingers across the enormous indentations in the soft ground beside him.

Neither man spoke until the road was once more under their feet. Wordsmith did not know what to say; Covenant needed nothing to say.

Wordsmith was never sure what kind of great animals had flanked him as he slept. He chose not to ask the beggar, lest he tell him not only what kind of animals but their very names as well. Even without that knowledge, the road gradually changed from a dusty ordeal into an unwinding revelation of the work and delights of the Elder God. And when they drew near to Glory, Wordsmith's world held more beauty than when they had left the village.

Only one sight arose which threatened to sap the joy from Wordsmith's revelations. From one point on the road, they could just see the edge of the village of the lepers. Covenant gazed upon it, but made no comment and did not move to alter his path toward the distant walls.

"This place is a misery," said Wordsmith.

"There is much misery here," answered Covenant. "I will send someone to ease their pain when the time is come."

"Is not this place ripe for a miracle? This, of all places?"

"No. There is suffering here, but there is no hope. Where there is no hope, there can be no miracle."

"There is a time for everything."

"That is a true saying, but you speak it lightly. Do you think the Elder God can look upon any place of suffering without sorrow?"

Wordsmith did not reply, and they moved on.

Later that afternoon, Covenant said, "We are nearly there."

Wordsmith had not, for the last few hours, even been thinking about Glory. His enthusiasm had vanished, but he answered, "Yes, I remember the road." He recalled the town clearly but with little warmth. He wondered what lay ahead for him now.

Even though Glory sat on a hill, travelers from the south came upon it suddenly. Even to those who lived there, it was always a surprise for the eyes. Covenant and Wordsmith turned the last bend in the road.

"Behold Glory, the center of all the earth," declared Wordsmith flatly.

"It is, even more than you can possibly imagine," answered Covenant.

From a distance, Glory seemed marvelous indeed. The high walls gleamed in the sunshine, and the roads led straight and immaculate through the many gates guarded by the massive white towers. The beginning of the maze of streets was just visible, masking the hills and springs, peaks and pools that Wordsmith knew lay within the walls. Glory was etched clearly in his mind. He knew the quiet areas where the houses stood grandly, far apart and almost isolated on broad streets, and the other parts where old crumbling buildings shouldered each other for air along tiny crooked passageways.

Deeper in, on its own triumphant hill, alone in its splendor, stood the palace of the Hermit King. Before and below the palace lay the Standing Stone, the Pool of Wealth, and the great amphitheater in the midst of the wonders where the Hermit King, upon rare occasion, addressed the inhabitants of Glory. Even though the palace lay within the walls, it was silent, still, and almost remote. Beyond the palace, beyond the walls and nestled in the hazy distance, more hills swept up to the foot of the Lonely Mountain—unclimbed and unclimbable, unknown and unknowable, shrouded in fog and wreathed in mist.

Covenant and Wordsmith continued to gaze at Glory. The donkey drifted aside and began to graze in the grass, being little impressed by the beauty of stones arranged by humans.

"You look as though you had never seen Glory before," said Wordsmith.

"I have seen it many times," the beggar replied. "I saw it before it was built—and I shall one day see it leveled." His eyes were moist, as he stood with folded arms. "I weep for Glory," he said, "and someday you will understand my tears."

"I understand the pain of illusions shattered," replied Wordsmith. "You cannot see the cracks and the corruption from this distance."

The beggar nodded. "Most who come here prefer not to notice. But for those who reject reality, the illusion is all they have, even if it exceeds the reality of the town. The eye will see what it believes it should see. But to me it is like seeing a living ghost, a ghost that does not yet know it is only a shadow. Once there was healing here. Now even the healing has died."

Wordsmith's eyes, gazing at the palace, betrayed his thoughts to his companion. Or perhaps he already knew them.

"Do you believe there will be an end to kings?" Covenant asked.

Wordsmith shrugged eloquently. "The king is old and heirless. Who will come after him?"

"Many wait in the shadows of the throne."

"Why should anyone want to be king? His men ensure the peace, but he does little besides. He is seldom seen and less frequently heard. He leaves us alone and is left alone. There is no circle of power in that throne, no tribute, no honor."

"Perhaps not to your mind. But is that the fault of this king, or the kings that have come and gone, or those who pretend to kneel before them? People are foolish, and will choose for themselves a king, even though they neither want nor intend to obey him."

The sun began to set behind them as they walked the last few miles into Glory, trailing the donkey behind them. The gates stood open, but attended. The guards did not stir at the travelers' approach; they were there to guard against wild animals, and at dusk they would close the gates behind them.

Covenant, Wordsmith, and Kingsburro walked directly beneath the archway into Glory. The town spread out before them in every direction. Wordsmith did not know whether to be elated or grieved. Glory held many memories for him; not all of them had been pleasant ones.

They walked a few hundred yards along the great broad street, and then Covenant stopped before a shop that displayed all manner of goods from the corners of the land. The curious, the rare, the unusual, the unobtainable were here. The shop was not large but, like many other shops, there were tiny rooms built above for living.

A peculiar carved sign was fastened over the door.

"Whose mark is that?" asked Wordsmith. "I have not seen it before."

"It is mine," answered Covenant, "fashioned with my own hands and hung here at my direction. This is the house of Candle," he continued. "It is our destination, for now."

There came a shout from within the shop. A few men and women came outside to meet them, eager to see Covenant but uncertain of the words to say.

Wordsmith saw a young man with an infant cradled in his arms; scars on his face were only partially hidden by a great billow of hair and the beginnings of a beard. A man and woman held hands, while an older woman hovered nearby.

Covenant introduced Wordsmith to them all. "Lionheart, with Woodswaif. Candle and Moonflower. Trueteller. This is Wordsmith. He too shall be one of us."

They greeted Wordsmith courteously, but their eyes returned again quickly to the beggar, showing both anxiety and awe, seeking more words from him.

"We came," said Candle.

"We waited," added Moonflower.

"We are here," announced Trueteller.

"And what shall we do now?" asked Lionheart.

"We should eat," said Covenant calmly. "Are we in time for the meal?"

They were. Trueteller, seeing her old friend the donkey, led him away behind the shop to the tiny stable where Roadreeler already dozed.

Covenant did not join in their conversation as they ate, and after the meal he disappointed them as well. "I will return by morning," he said. "Wait for me here, all of you." Then he was gone, absorbed into the river of people flowing through the streets.

Lionheart eventually broke the awkward silence, as Woodswaif lay gurgling and content at his feet. "We have been living in the rooms above Candle's shop," he said to Wordsmith. "We have prepared a bed for you as well."

"Thank you. Will Covenant sleep here as well?" asked Wordsmith.

"I do not know where he will sleep," said Candle.

"Or even if he does," added Moonflower. "He is a man of many strange powers."

"Who *is* he?" asked Lionheart.

Shyly, they began to tell each other their stories before the kitchen fire, with the absent Covenant present in the midst of all their words. Shyness thawed in the warmth of strange things revealed, and laughter came. After the laughter came yawning and sleep, and then puzzled peace reigned in the house of Candle.

Only Trueteller was still awake when the beggar returned. "Covenant?" she asked, trying unsuccessfully to sleep in the massive wooden chair. "This is very crowded and uncomfortable. How many more do you intend to gather under your wings?"

"I will multiply this company many times. But I also assure you they will not have to squeeze into this house."

"Then where? There is no place in Glory to hold a multitude all at once."

Covenant nodded, smiling. "Then we must build one."

SEVEN

This
Shall Be
My House

THE NEXT AFTERNOON, COVENANT GATHERED THE COMpany of those he had called, saying, "The time has come to build my house." At Covenant's bidding, Candle shuttered the shop and they all trailed after him into Glory.

Trueteller carried Woodswaif, but only because she actually had hips, and Lionheart was far too lean and bony to offer a comfortable perch for the baby. Nevertheless, his eyes rarely left her for long.

They left the streets of shops behind them and slowly passed from prosperity into poverty, winding their way deeper into parts of Glory neither Wordsmith nor Candle recognized. The streets narrowed and filled with old clutter and shadows. Rats (or something else small and ferocious) scuttled in the gutters. The walkers drew close to one another, and closest of all to Covenant, though they saw few people. Many of the buildings had fallen from neglect or from the shaking and sinking of the ground, and they had been ransacked for stone and brick and wood. Those buildings which had not altogether crumbled were too quiet, conveying only hopelessness.

Covenant halted them all before one of the grandest ruins of all.

From the outside, it looked like the other dusty stone shells, stained with age and marked with neglect. There were no doors or windows left intact. Inside they saw nothing but rubble. How the walls continued to stand was a mystery; though the stones were thick and solid, and their mortar still held firmly, there were only a few cracked beams left to brace them.

The small company mounted the ruined steps and entered the gaping doorway—Covenant boldly, the rest with caution. They stood in vacancy and watched the walls crumble.

"You shall live here?" queried Wordsmith. His whispered words echoed from one bare stone wall to another.

"We all shall!" claimed Covenant, his words waking brighter echoes.

"This is only a shell from which the life has flown," said Trueteller.

"Then life has come to it again," answered Covenant.

"What was this place?" asked Lionheart.

"At an ancient time," Covenant said, "it was a holy house to the Elder God. But he was neglected, and then forgotten. This building has met a similar fate."

"And what shall we do with it?" asked Trueteller.

"We shall rebuild it with our own hands."

Covenant's words were met by shocked silence.

Wordsmith eventually found his voice. "There is little left here to build with but rubble. This is a ruin—all that can be carried away *has* been carried away."

"At least it is honest rubble. And it was once holy, hewn from the hearts of the mountains and carried here with the sacrifice of sweat."

"Why did they build here?"

Covenant ushered them to the edge of an old pit that sank down along one wall. "Many times before us there have been seekers here who followed rumors of treasure. Someone has dug by this wall, quitting when they reached the great rocks." They all could see the stones, too deep in the earth and far too vast to have been quarried and moved by human beings. "The seekers left, disappointed, not knowing they had found a great treasure indeed." Covenant, working his way deeper into the pit, knocked his fist against one of the massive stones. At his touch the rock boomed with a deep softness like a solid bronze bell, an element of the earth that lived but could not be moved.

"These stones," said Covenant when the echoes had faded, "are the last foundations of the City that once was here and shall be again. They are old—not carved by human hands—and part of the rock that has always been here. People guessed long ago—and dug and delved in the earth, and they were allowed to find this foundation—that they might build this temple. But in the ages that followed, they forgot what they had found. Or at least they ceased to understand it.

"Here, indeed, was the gate to the City," Covenant continued. "What was left behind has been removed, and what people built after their own fashion has fallen. We will build on this very place once more, and we will use the stones that are here."

"Covenant," said Lionheart, "this is far too grand for a handful of people."

"There will be others." Covenant smiled a smile that was born in a nest of good secrets.

"Others? Are they all following you to Glory?"

"No, there are others whom I have called, but not called to be here. Not yet. And there are many whom I shall call, either

to come or to go. And the more I call, the more room there shall be, until we have many, and all have enough."

"How are we to build such a place?" asked Candle. "We have no army at hand."

"We are enough," answered Covenant. "You need do only the tasks I give you—the jobs that lie to your hands to do. The other work will follow. There is a very old saying you all should ponder: *Complete the possible, and the impossible will follow.*"

Covenant would say nothing more. They followed him back to Candle's house for the night, where he left them again to carry out his lone and unspoken pursuits.

The next morning, they came together to the empty stone shell to begin their work. Covenant divided their labors immediately. Trueteller and Lionheart began to scrape the drifted earth from the tiles, with Woodswaif in a basket on the floor between them. Moonflower and Candle pulled weeds and shrubs that had grown unwanted but unheeded in the corners. And Wordsmith stacked splintered blocks and bricks collected from the floor.

Uncalled urchins gathered behind them and played in the far corners. There were mocking words, but Covenant did not chase them away.

None of the others aided Wordsmith with his appointed task, but it seemed to him that unseen helpers worked behind his back. The stack grew much faster than he had imagined possible. And the blocks, when he bent to inspect them again, no longer seemed so fragile. The corners were square and firm, where moments before there had been only weakness, air, and crumbling stone.

"Covenant?" he called, not sure how to express his wonder in words.

If he was listening, Covenant was not answering. He spoke to Lionheart and Trueteller instead. "Wash these slabs," Covenant suggested, "and see if more than the dirt comes away."

Their efforts were rewarded immediately. Where they

scrubbed, the pits and cracks seemed to come away with the sponge, leaving the floor whole and smooth and glossy once more.

"This is not an ordinary house," said Trueteller.

"It was never meant to be," answered Covenant.

Later that day, Candle beckoned the beggar aside. "Covenant, what of my shop? How can I serve both you and my customers? Is this to be my home as well, that I must work upon it?"

"Your business is doing well."

Candle was not sure whether Covenant had answered the question, asked one of his own, or merely made a statement.

"Yes," he agreed, to be safe.

"Then let it close for a few days. It will do even better as you learn from me, working with us. When you begin to see people as more than their money, people will come to you in loyalty and friendship as well as in trade. You shall keep your shop, and you will find that your shop will keep itself. You will indeed come to live here, for you will soon need all your present rooms above for your wares. There will be abundant room for the three of you here."

So the days passed, and the house continued to grow beneath their hands. Each had a task, though the task changed from day to day. They often worked in pairs and multiplied their labor, each one wondering if the other was doing extra work unseen. And each night, they slept the sleep of the righteously tired.

Yet there were parts of the house that Wordsmith never labored on, nor did anyone else that he could discern. The shell of a great five-sided tower still loomed above the back of the house, and it was being restored day by day with no obvious labor invested.

It was several days before Wordsmith realized that the tower was apparently being rebuilt from the top down. Wordsmith could see the work progressing far above him, yet there were no stairs or ladders within or without by which one could reach the work. Wordsmith could not have wandered there, even if he had so chosen.

He inquired about the tower's progress, but Covenant only said that the tower was not ready for others to see. "You shall be the first of the few who will see it, for it is being built for you. This tower reaches rare heights. It cannot be climbed by just any man."

There were many other things Wordsmith could not explain. He was never quite certain how the mammoth beams had been relaid for the floors, nor was he sure of their origin. The oak columns had simply been there on the ground one day; if anyone had actually lifted them into place, Wordsmith could not determine who it was.

A maze of walls had slowly grown within, and there seemed to be no end to all the rooms. Wordsmith was convinced they had not built so many as he now found. He had carved and carried doors himself, but not this many. The wood was darker and richer than he remembered, and he traced his fingers along the delicate embellishments and wondered how he had even imagined them, much less fashioned them himself.

Wordsmith toiled patiently, continuing to watch the tower. And at last, one afternoon, he saw that the stairs now reached the ground. He began to look for Covenant, but Covenant found him first.

"Your touch can be seen in any room of this house," said the beggar, "but not here. This tower has been made for you, and you alone. You could not work on it, for it is empowered beyond your capacity to gift it. It required the touch of my hands. You have labored enough on the house. Now I will give you a different task—more difficult, more demanding, less common. The steps to the tower, and the tower itself, are finished. Let us climb together."

Wordsmith paused with one foot on the lowest stair. "You have not asked me to sing since I returned to Glory," he stated.

"No, I have not."

"Shall I ever sing again at your command?"

"For now, it is my command that you refrain from singing. You thought your voice was your gift to the world, but it is not. You shall indeed sing again, but not alone. Now is not the time to sing; it is the time to see and think and do and write. I have other voices to sing for me—some which you have heard already, but do not know it. I have only you to write down the tales of the City."

They ascended the stairway.

Several hours later, Covenant descended alone. "You will not see Wordsmith again for several days," he told the others, "but all is well. He has begun a new task."

Before many more sunsets had passed, the others finished their tasks without him. Proud, hot, and happy, they stood in the cool street with Covenant and rested in their handiwork.

"Surely we did not do this work," said Trueteller. "It is far too fine for the fruit of hands such as mine." The others agreed. "Shall we repair the outside now?" she asked Covenant. "The inside is ready."

Covenant shook his head slowly. "No," he said, "we shall not. Whatever is outside now, let it be as man has left it. Whatever is inside, let it be beautiful and clean. This house shall become known for what is inside it, and not for its own appearance. Let the world that looks for outer beauty look elsewhere."

"What shall we do now?" asked Candle.

"Let us clean the last dirt away from beneath our feet," answered Covenant. "Then the need will present itself."

The others began to sweep the steps for a final time, while Candle moved to the far side of the door to stack extra lumber.

As she swept, Moonflower brushed away a drift of wood shavings and shrieked with surprise and delight. She scooped something from the dirt and yelled to Candle, "I found your pledge!"

He, moving aside an armload of wood, gave her a like

answer: "And I have found your half!"

They met on the stairs, sharing their speechlessness and matching their medallions.

Only after a moment did Moonflower say, "Candle? These cannot be ours! Look at our names here!"

"They are our names," he said, not comprehending.

"They are our *new* names," she replied simply.

And then Candle was struck by another realization. "And these are gold, not silver. What does this mean?"

"Do you remember when Covenant asked us what we had lost—and then he spoke those words about our pledges? He called them 'silver ornaments.' But how did he know they were silver? He never saw them."

They turned to Covenant, who stood amused at the bottom of the steps. "What is the meaning of this?" asked Candle, holding the divided gold medallion high.

"It is the answer to the question as to what we should do with this house," Covenant announced. "First we shall have a wedding."

EIGHT

The Book
& the
Burden

YOU HAVE GIVEN ME WONDERFUL TALES TO WRITE," WORD-smith said, looking at the piles of parchment littered on the table. He stood and stretched, as if to throw off the weight of the night. "Now I must turn and tell them again. But who will listen?"

Covenant looked at him from his seat beside the table. "There are hungry hearts and willing ears here in Glory, as well as all the villages beyond. You cannot count them—but I can, and have. I know that they are waiting for your words, though some will not know what their hunger is until it has been satisfied."

"My heart is so full that it quivers," said Wordsmith.

"Are you weary?" Covenant asked.

"My eyes are tired, and my arms are tired, and my back is

tired, but my heart and mind will never tire of this."

"Is that all that pains you?"

"My stomach aches as well."

"You have missed many meals," remarked Covenant. "Your body needs food as much as your heart."

Wordsmith nodded, motioning to the five great windows in the room. "Day comes and goes, night follows and fades, but all time seems the same up here when I watch the fifth window: From the other windows I can indeed see in all directions, but I cannot see straight down. What is happening below?"

"My house is finished. You are sitting now at the crown of the beggar's haven."

"Have I been here that long?" asked Wordsmith, astonished.

"Long enough," said Covenant. "This house is ready, and a wedding feast is being prepared."

Wordsmith did not seem surprised.

"It is time," continued Covenant. "They have waited long for this and worked hard for it. Now that your present burst of imagination is spent, you should descend among us again. There is work to be done there as well."

"What manner of work?"

"If you are to preside over this house, you must see what it is you are steward of."

"Steward? *This* task is enough!"

"Does not the work with the pen delight you?"

"Yes," Wordsmith said, "more than I ever thought, though it exhausts me as well. Before, my singing was all that I ever wanted to do. But you know how I fared in Glory when I came to sing."

Covenant nodded.

Wordsmith turned toward the windows. "I was nothing here—a good but untrained voice among many both fine and trained. My betters wrestled with one another to gain a few coppers singing in the inns. What chance had I? I came, and I failed."

"But you did come, and you did dare your dream. Not many have done even that. Besides, not all failure is evil. One must test doors to see if they are unlatched. One must follow some paths to see if they lead anywhere at all. And your failure has honed you for the task I have set ahead of you. Only a man who has known the death of a dream will be strong enough to survive the days ahead."

"What do you mean?"

"I will tell you more at another time, when you have been made more ready."

"Must I be made and remade again? You seem to be always shaping me."

"It is not that I am making of you a different man. I am only remolding the man who was there from the beginning. You have been growing away from yourself all these years, and now it is time to grow back. You were born for these stories, and not for singing. You shall sing again, but not for the crowds, not for honor, not for Glory. You shall sing again, but for love and for love alone. Until then, you will have the stories that come to you here in the tower."

"The stories—" Wordsmith began. He paused, then began again in earnest. "In every story there is good against evil. But where does evil come from? I do not mean simply greed and selfishness and a bent to pleasure, or stupidity and fear and sloth. I can find those in my own heart without any help. But where does the higher evil come from? Why do we make slaves of each other, and agree together in cold blood to destroy and ravage? Why are children cruel and women cold? Why do our hopes fail us? Why does the world grow darker every year?"

"You have seen the story of the City," replied the beggar, "and written it down. Do you recall the one who played strange music in the wilderness and drew people away from the One who had made them? That one is still alive; I know him by one name—Twister—though he is known by many

79

names. His only desire is to destroy, and to rule over that destruction. So far, he has been prevented." Covenant smiled an odd smile, as though he were thinking of other times and other places far away in distance and remote in time. "He is old—older than you can imagine. In all those ages he has become very clever, but he has not become wise. You should look to him for the root of all evil."

"Has he put blackness in the hearts of all everywhere?"

"He planted those dark seeds in everyone whom he lured away from the safety of the City. He has done the same with everyone born into this world since."

"But has he so corrupted you?" asked Wordsmith.

"No." Covenant smiled again. "He does not have that power."

"But why should Twister do all these things?"

"Why should he not? There is none to stop him but the Elder God. It is Twister's chosen nature to sow evil. After all, it was Twister who opened the fateful path into the wilderness, with full knowledge of what could follow."

"So he is my enemy as well as yours."

"Yes, but he is far too strong for you. Do not confront him."

"Is he too strong for any of us?"

"He is stronger than any person who now walks this earth."

"Is he stronger even than you?"

"You will think so, when the time comes."

"But who shall conquer him? When will the Elder God cry halt to this evil?"

"You shall have to wait for the voiceless child. But do not be dismayed at anything that comes before; Twister will indeed win many battles—but he cannot win the final war."

"Covenant," said Wordsmith, after a moment's reflection, "I have asked you many questions this morning. Yet I am still confused, for you have answered none of them directly."

"Do my answers seem more like deeper riddles?" he asked as he stood and beckoned Wordsmith down the winding stairs.

"They *are* answers, but you are unable to hear them. Remember that *I* am your answer, in and of myself. I need not answer any of your questions, but I have chosen to do so. And now I have given you all the answers that will fit in your mind. Come and eat, and then you and I will survey this house."

They went immediately. At the end of two hours, Wordsmith's legs were weary, and he sat heavily on a chair in one of the backstairs rooms. Covenant stood lightly beside him, untired by the many stairs they had climbed and the rooms and passages they had explored.

"I do not understand where all this splendor came from," said Wordsmith.

"You all built it with your own hands."

Wordsmith shook his head. "Not this. This is grand beyond our imagining, exquisite beyond our skills. There is nothing lacking."

"Everything that is needful is here," said Covenant. "Tables, chairs, beds, clothing, dishes, pots . . ."

"I do not know where you brought it all from," said Wordsmith.

"I will someday soon show you more of this house's deeper secrets."

He handed Wordsmith an ornate key on a chain. "There is only one key," he said, "for there is only one lock in this house."

"The door to the street?"

"That door has no lock, for it is open to all at all times."

"Do you not fear thieves?"

"A thief is only a threat if your treasures can be stolen," he replied. "The lock is on the single door you have not yet seen— the door which leads to the path which leads to the City."

"The pathway is *here?*"

"Yes, as I promised."

"What is it like?" Wordsmith asked quietly.

"You shall see for yourself, directly. Come. We have one last

adventure this day. The path inward to the City is not difficult; the difficult part is coming back. I will give you that
choice. But I warn you: No matter whether you say yes or no
to my offer before the City, you will never be the same again."

"Will it be a good change?"

"One leads to the best of all possible changes—and the other
leads to something even better."

"Then I am not afraid."

Covenant led Wordsmith down the hall to the final door.

— NINE —

Proven
Metal

T HAT EVENING WORDSMITH ATE SILENTLY AT THE TABLE, his mind far away in worlds no one else could yet imagine.

"Wordsmith?" asked Trueteller. "Are you all right?"

"I don't know," he answered abstractedly. "This has not been an ordinary day."

"What day of ours has been ordinary since the beggar came to us?"

"If I could put into words what I have seen today, you would not believe me."

"I would believe almost anything," she replied. "Remember, I have seen the once-dead burst forth from the grave."

Covenant stepped into the room, looking for them. "Come," he said, "There are proclamations to be made in this place."

Wordsmith and Trueteller followed him to the great hall

where Candle and Moonflower stood beaming at each other and waiting for the company to gather. Lamps and candles stood in every available space, and the house was awash with soft light in the dusk.

The newcomers took pillowed chairs (where Lionheart already held Woodswaif), and Covenant moved to stand between Candle and Moonflower and in front of them all.

"First," he said, "I proclaim Wordsmith as the steward of this my house. I shall not always be here, and when I am away he will speak for me. I have shown him the ways of this house and the wisdom hidden in it, and each day he gains more. He—and under him you all—shall administer comfort, serve food, and offer shelter to any who have need of it."

They applauded Wordsmith, though he did not know how to accept their praise for something he had only begun to do. To his relief, they soon came to the second proclamation.

In solemn joy they all watched as Moonflower and Candle matched the tokens once more. They spoke then the words of promise that would bind them to one another. Afterward, Covenant took the rendered metal pledges from their hands and held them high in his right fist and invoked the name of the Elder God. There was a flash of golden flame. When he drew down his hand and opened his fingers, his palm held two complete medallions on gold chains. "Place this one around her neck," Covenant directed Candle. "And place this one around his," he told Moonflower. When the two performed their actions, he smiled at them and said, "Now you belong to each other."

After the ceremony, they all ate at their leisure, and laughed much, and cried some, and talked at length of the new futures that had been given to each one of them by the beggar. Woodswaif fell asleep on Lionheart's shoulder; he would not lay her down, and so he ate as best he could with only one hand.

Moonflower and Candle held each other close, and Moonflower fitted her face against her husband's neck. After a moment she pulled back and held up his medallion for him to see. "Look," she said, "There is a new marking on the back. Covenant's mark."

"I am no longer surprised by anything he does," murmured Candle, "but he has brought us nothing but good."

Later, Covenant led the pair upstairs to a set of rooms they had not seen before, where there were chairs and lamps and pillows and a curtained bed. And there Covenant left them to each other, while he returned to the feast below.

TEN

The Woes
of the
World

DRAWN BY A MISERY EVEN GREATER THAN HIS OWN, A hunchback staggered down the tangled back streets of Glory. Every twitch of his muscles betrayed his pain. His face was an uplifted agony, and all his bones were warped.

Yet where he stopped and touched the sufferers in the shadows, their pain paled and healing came and lingered, and the unseen weight on the hunchback's shoulders grew heavier. With each pause and each touch he groaned anew, but said nothing else aloud.

The hunchback crept along the gutter and humped to a stop in front of one of the undistinguished structures in the dry backwaters of the human wash. The house was old and tall and once grand. Now it was tattered on the outside, though still kept clean.

A beggar sat on the step of the house and eyed the hunchback. "I have been waiting for you," said the beggar. "I could feel you drawing near."

"I have come to take away your pain," said the hunchback.

"Then you have come in vain," answered Covenant. "Indeed, you carry the woes of the world, but you cannot carry mine. And now your strength is gone. You must rest here in this house if you hope to take another step in this life."

Weary and surprised by his own rising weakness, the hunchback nodded and began to obey the beggar's summons. But he could walk no farther, and he collapsed in a twisted ruin on the street. Men came at the beggar's call to carry the fallen one inside.

Later, the hunchback drifted up through clouds of horrid encoiling dreams to find himself in bed. The bedroom was not splendid or elaborate, but it was clean and sweet smelling. A thick woolen blanket covered him, and he had not at first the strength to pull it back. He turned his head slowly and saw the beggar sitting patiently in the corner.

"Welcome to my house," said the beggar. "My name is Covenant."

"And my name is best forgotten," croaked the hunchback, turning his face toward the wall.

"You may let it fade, if it pleases you. I will not call you by the name with which you were born."

"Few know that name."

"Few do," Covenant agreed.

"That name is a curse. Do not shame me with it again. I have no name. I need no name. I am nameless."

"You are not nameless. Every being has a name, whether it knows it or not."

Silence ruled the room until the hunchback murmured his first question. "What manner of house is this?"

"This is an ancient and honorable house," said Covenant. "It is only from the outside that it seems ancient and dishonorable."

The hunchback flinched at the word *dishonorable*, but Covenant continued without pausing. "I know you, I know your gift, and I know as well what goads you on."

"You are a healer too," whispered the hunchback, struggling to push back the blanket and sit up. "I can feel it."

"We heal for different reasons, perhaps. A man can be motivated by more than compassion. You are a driven man," said Covenant. "I have need for you in my service. The weak and wounded come here daily and have need of help."

"I must stay, it seems," the hunchback answered, "unless you carry me back to the door. If I can help you, I will."

Covenant nodded, content. He rose to leave, and then said, "Since you acknowledge no particular name, I shall give you a new one: Woebearer. You have been Woebearer for many; I shall do the same for you, when you have confessed the second half of the great secret. You have discovered that you may bear the sorrows of another, but you have not yet discovered that you cannot bear your own."

Covenant met Wordsmith outside the door, who pulled him aside. "This man does not belong here. He is ignorant of you and does no work in your name."

"He does all his work in my name," rejoined Covenant, "though neither he nor you realize it. Let him remain and let him heal, that he may heal again. He hurts no one and helps all. He will learn the needful lessons when his time is come."

"Who is he?" pressed Wordsmith. "How is he doing this? What warps him so?"

"He has done a foolish evil in his life and caused much suffering under another name. He thinks in vain that if he wrests enough suffering from the backs of others and carries it himself, he will be set free from the distress of his own guilt. But those are chains he cannot break and can never shed unaided, no matter the strength in his hands. Remember the rule of this house," Covenant added. "It does not matter what he has done. It matters what he will be."

"And what will he be?"

"You shall see soon enough."

The beggar's words came true with the dawn. A renewed Woebearer bounded downstairs to Covenant's table, clutched the beggar's shoulder, and cried, "Look! Last night, while I slept . . ."

Wordsmith and the others at table stared at the transformation. The work of the night was plain: the intolerable weight on the man's shoulders had been lifted. His back was almost straight, and his pain had receded. His face had straightened now, though still grooved with the tracks of old tears, and some of his bones had unbowed.

He was the same man, but he was not the same man.

Woebearer continued his incredible tale. "Last night, for the first time in many years, I had no dreams!"

"You mean you had no nightmares," countered Covenant calmly.

"They are all the same to me."

"You will soon remember the difference," promised Covenant.

"How did this happen? Is this a magic house?"

Wordsmith answered first. "This is indeed a magic house. I am no longer startled by any good thing that happens here."

"Was this *your* doing?" Woebearer asked Covenant directly.

"Yes," Covenant said. "You would have died had your burdens not been lifted from you. You have worn your body to the very bone by following the trail of others' miseries. The shadow of death hovered over you even as you paused at this door."

"But now I am not dying!"

"You are still dying, but much more slowly now. Your death has only been delayed. I will not take your gift from you, even though I believe it is more your burden than your blessing. But you will not survive yourself on your mission unless you sleep here each night and eat the food that is served at my table."

"I cannot leave?"

"You may leave any time you like," said Covenant, nodding to the streets. "If you are a prisoner here, you are a prisoner of your own need to be needed. Here, and here alone, will you find untroubled sleep and the nightly lifting of your burdens. If you leave this house to wander again you will surely die, and you will suffer evil dreams until you do."

The hunchback pondered. "If," he said, "if I go and draw another load of misery, would I be healed again tonight?"

"You may."

"Then I must go and see!" Woebearer leaped up and plunged out the door into the streets again.

"Will he be back?" asked Wordsmith in the sudden hush.

"He will be back," answered Covenant. "He believes he has found paradise here. He is right, but for all the wrong reasons."

ELEVEN

The Bright Flower

SHE WAS BEAUTIFUL AND HAD LONG BEEN DESIRED ABOVE all other women in Glory. Her likeness bloomed in drawings hung on a thousand walls, and her image hovered in the hearts of many men.

Her name was Beauty, and word of her footsteps in the streets swept on before her, drawing watchers from all manner of people. Among those who came to see were Covenant and Woebearer.

Covenant turned his face toward hers, and she saw it first among all the crowd. It was not a remarkable visage, but it drew her. And then she saw the contorted face and body of Woebearer, and in fascination she continued to stare. Covenant was not waving or cheering or trying to attract her attention. He was merely gazing at her and smiling. But his eyes compelled her to return his gaze.

She should know him, she thought. He looked at her without appraising her—an incident that disturbed her at first. She could not readily break its power. For a moment, in all that crowd she could see only the two men.

"She too carries much pain," said Woebearer, "but it is sorrow and loneliness, not suffering."

"There is more to come," answered Covenant. "She has not yet been abandoned."

Then there appeared another face to draw her eye away: a handsome gentleman, standing at ease across the street from Covenant and Woebearer.

"We are not alone," said Covenant. "He, too, has come to behold this Beauty."

Beauty passed on, and the crowd melted away, leaving only the three men on the street.

"You know this man?" asked Woebearer.

"He is my enemy," replied Covenant, "and therefore yours as well. In everything I do, he opposes me. And in everything he does, I oppose him. We have met before. We shall meet again many times."

"Soon?" Woebearer wondered. "Now?"

"Later. Much later. You see, his plan is to rule Glory. He must be content with that, for the way to the City is forever closed to him. He lived there, once, and was exiled to this land until the City reappears. And then he will be judged. Once he was the keeper of the door. It bitters him now, for there are marks on the door where we struggled, he and I. I cast him down and banished him from my house."

Woebearer pondered. "What is his name?"

"He has many. Some know him as Twister, others as Fame or Fortune, or Mesmer, Mummer—whatever suits his purpose. But you see, I know his true name."

The air chilled momentarily. Twister—or whoever was behind that name—turned suddenly and stalked off.

Later that same morning, Wordsmith pressed his way

through the crowd around Beauty and presented her with a book. "These words were written for you," he said. Beauty, who had received many such tributes, nevertheless thanked him graciously and glanced politely at the first few pages. When he had gone, she gave the book to one of her attendants, and promptly eased the memories of all four men from her mind.

None of the four men forgot her.

TWELVE

The
Wondrous
Wine

T HE FALL DEEPENS," SAID COVENANT, LOOKING OUT THE
door past the streets of Glory, "and I have a promise to keep."

"To my people?" Wordsmith stood near the fire.

"To your people. The drought has nearly slain them, and
when the snow comes, they will have no grain. And no hope
for more." He gathered their cloaks from the peg by the mantel. "And now is the season before the snow. We will be in
time if we go now."

The two left the warm house behind and turned from Glory
over the falling leaves, the one walking slowly to keep pace
with the other's uneven steps.

"We came to Glory by the short and lonely way, where few
tread. We shall return to your village by the long and winding
way, where people live. When we journeyed before, we talked

much and kept our own counsel. Now we have other tasks to do, other reasons to be on the road."

"Will I always walk like this?" asked Wordsmith wistfully, after a few halting miles.

"Some day you shall run again, like these leaves before the wind. I know my kindness bewilders you, but I ask you to be content and patient. Some day you will understand. You have accomplished much this summer," he added.

"And I have learned more."

"That is why you have accomplished much."

When the day's light failed them at last, they sheltered in a town that had little food to spare.

"The drought," the innkeeper explained. "It has destroyed us. There is no water in the river that flows from the mountains. Our grain and fruit wither in the fields. Nor is there any grain from the west this year. The Elder God has failed us. He no longer hears our prayers."

"Do you still have one who intercedes at his altar? I saw the stone as we entered the town."

"Yes. The head man of the village prays there daily. He is the one who has kept our faith alive."

"In the morning, as soon as there is enough light to tell one face from another, you should find him and bring him to meet us at the altar. And bring the people of the village as well." Leaving the puzzled innkeeper in their wake, Wordsmith and the beggar went gratefully to bed.

And in the morning, before the dawn, they rose and walked slowly out of doors to the altar. The innkeeper joined them within a few minutes, drawing behind him an old man still banishing sleep from his eyes. "I had a dream," he was saying, "a dream of harvest and good fruits on the edge of winter. There was a beggar carrying grain, and a cripple laden with ripe fruit. They came to our village—"

He saw the travelers, and stopped and stared.

The beggar spoke first. "Behold, old man of durable faith.

Your daydream stands before you. Are our images fresh in your mind? Then hear us, for we come in the name of the Elder God."

The old man spread wide his arms. "We are at your mercy. And at your service."

The beggar looked around at the growing crowd. "If you would see the end of this drought, then command each man in all the village to scour every house and bring me the grain— the whole grain, the kernel, everything that has not been ground between the stones. Put it here, before the altar." The old man moved, and ordered, and the two travelers had but to stand and watch the baskets and pots of grain grow at their feet. There was not much to be gathered.

"Is this all?" Wordsmith asked. "You may forfeit the blessing if you withhold any." The old man gazed into all the faces about him, questioning, until a woman flushed red and withdrew a tiny pouch from the pocket of her cloak. She tossed it on the pile, and the sad rebellion in her eyes declared it to be her all.

"Place it all in two sacks," the beggar ordered. And two sacks were filled, each one no more than a fair burden for a strong man. "You have fruit still?" he asked. "Enough for three days? Then keep it, and share it generously among yourselves. We shall take these sacks with us, and in three days your harvest will be upon you." He handed one sack to Wordsmith and led the way to the westward road. Despair came to roost in the village, but at the word of the old man no one stood in their way.

"Three days," he muttered to himself. "Three days. Grant us the strength for such a span of hours."

Out on the road, Wordsmith asked, "And what of their harvest? I do not understand. Is this all?"

"No," the beggar said, "it is not."

The day grew hot again, and Covenant and Wordsmith grew quickly tired with the burdens of grain on their back. The arrow-straight, shadeless road had driven thirst into their

throats, and they had long since shed their cloaks. The squat, shabby, stone-and-mud structure before them was neither pleasant nor inviting, but it was the only travelers' shelter they had seen for miles. A few old men and children panted in its shade, their faces and tongues as dusty as the weathered way.

"Have you any water here?" asked Covenant.

"We have waterskins and wooden barrels, jars and bottles to spare," said one of the men, "but we have no water. The long drought has left us nothing fit for the mouth of any living being, save the wine inside—and it is too dear to drink. We have only ancient mud, and our merchant has only aged wine."

"You are thirsty?" another man asked with a knowing smile.

"We are," replied Covenant. "Though possibly not so thirsty as you have been."

"Then I shall warn you that the keeper here is a very rude and greedy man. He will not even notice you unless he sees the gleam of your coppers."

"I have a few coppers in my bag," said Covenant. "And if there is no water, then we must drink the wine instead. He will not share?"

"He will only sell."

"Perhaps I can change his mind."

The two travelers entered, and the rest came after, hoping that inside was cooler than the shade, thinking that perhaps a wanderer would share what a merchant would not.

"Bring me a cup of your best!" commanded Covenant, rattling a few coins down the length of the first wooden table.

The merchant brought a bottle of wine and a cup, with many praises for its taste and clarity. "This is a truly wonderful wine!"

Covenant drank, and then put the cup down with a gesture of irritation. "Is this what passes for wine here?" he asked. "It tastes like water to me."

"Here—let me taste it," barked the merchant. He snatched the cup away and swallowed a mouthful. Surprised, he spat it out and poured another cup from the long bottle. It, too, was only water. "Take this away!" cried the merchant, as he disappeared into his cellar again.

"The boy will do it for you," called Covenant after the confounded man. He beckoned to one of the children in the doorway—a boy who looked to the beggar to be wise beyond his years. "Take this outside and dispose of it properly." The boy eagerly lifted the bottle off the table and lugged it outside. Covenant winked, and some of the others followed the boy, new smiles concealed under the dust of the day.

The merchant returned with more wine, uttering great apologies and greater promises.

Covenant tasted again, and his face filled with disappointment. "Take this, too, away." Covenant waved the second bottle outside with one hand and dazzled the merchant with the clink of coppers in his other.

"You test the next bottle, Wordsmith," said the beggar quietly.

It, too, was only water—as were the next ten bottles. They all had a chance to test the vintage. On the point of collapse, the merchant asked frantically of the heavens, "Is all my wine ruined?"

"It cannot be ruined," said Covenant, "if it is not wine." He stood up. "Keep the coppers. You have found us no wine, but you have, at length, quenched our thirst."

"But there is still one bottle . . ." his voice trailed off into uncertain silence.

"Here are more coppers," Covenant responded. "You shall keep this last bottle—whether of wine or of water—until I send for it. Keep it there upon the mantel where all can see and ask their questions, but keep it safe and unhandled."

"How will I know when you need it?" the confused merchant queried.

"I will send a boy for it, and he shall bear this token." Covenant plucked up the top coin on the pile of coppers and snapped it in two like a withered leaf. "He shall bear the other half of this coin." He tossed the broken copper to the dazed merchant, who could only stare wordlessly as they left.

Outside, Covenant remarked to Wordsmith, "That was truly a wonderful wine. See? No one is thirsty now."

THIRTEEN

Before
Winter

WHEN THE TWO TRAVELERS CAME AT LAST TO WORD-smith's village, they found that hunger had settled there before them. The few people left behind came to meet them with smiles, fear, and many words—words of waiting, of drought, of hardship, of rejoicing.

"We ate the last food yesterday," they complained. "It was hard to await you. We feared the snow would come before you."

"You see that it has not, though clouds follow hard upon us. Have all waited?"

"No. There were four who left. But we did as you said, and we have purchased their land." The one who spoke showed him the deeds.

"You have done well." The beggar opened one of the sacks.

"And here is grain."

"You have brought us food! But how will it be enough? And for how long?"

"It is not to eat. Not now. You have believed that the hard part of your trial was to wait—but now I ask you to do a harder thing yet." He called the people to arrange themselves by families and come forward. To each person—child, woman and man—he gave a handful of grain. "Take this to your fields and scatter the grain. All of it. Spread it in equal measures upon the good soil and the sour, upon the untouched earth and the scorched. Do not withhold any of it, nor eat of it, nor bring a single seed back with you."

They went, all of them, save Wordsmith and the beggar. "I begin to see," said Wordsmith, "the depth of your ways. I shall write of this, too."

"You shall."

The two men stood, then, and silently watched the sowers.

When each family returned, the beggar asked them, "Have you obeyed my word? Have you scattered it all, without judging the ground?" They all answered him alike. And when they all were done and night was falling, he bade them build a fire in the square and sleep around it.

Rain came in the night, soft rain, falling only in the fields and coming not into the village. No lightning flickered in its midst. The sound of the waters was music to the withered land.

And in the morning the people beheld great waves of grain about them, and they ran rejoicing into the golden depths. The beggar followed and moved among them, taking each one aside and reminding them that the land was now theirs in everlasting trust, and that none should take it away save the Elder God. And he bade them remember how it was that the land had first been given and then taken from those who had not devoted the firstfruits.

He came to one man who stood bewildered in his field. The

grain had grown there, but not tall, and there were many patches of bare ground. The man turned his troubled face to the beggar, who watched him with sad eyes.

"Your grain would have been like the others had you obeyed me. But you held back the grain, you or your family."

The man nodded mutely.

"Small is the price of your lesson. You will have enough here for your needs. But not until the next harvest will you have any to spare or sell."

He gathered the people together and brought them back to the square. "You have learned the way of the covenant. You have taken humility upon your shoulders. You have obeyed, and I have spared your fields and homes and goods. I made the proud and greedy and unyielding your benefactors, for now you own what they labored for. But you, too, will be unable to hold it if you neglect the old laws and forget the Elder God.

"Your faith has been rewarded. But there are others in the land this night who have given their faith and have not their answer. Not one of you has asked me where this grain came from. It was a gift from others—given to you in my name, at my command. They have blessed you, and it is time that you bless them. Take buckets, all of you, and pots and pails and wineskins. Fill them here at the well and follow me to the river."

They assembled again at the riverbed, still dry now where once rainbows had rippled in running waters.

Wordsmith asked Covenant, "Why is there water in the fields, and not here?"

"It is not here because it all fell in the fields," he answered.

Then the beggar beckoned the man whose faith had wavered as he sowed. "Pour your bucket into the river, and then return for more. And the rest of you after him."

Then he sat beside Wordsmith on the riverbank and watched the procession. Many looked in wonder at the beggar, and one called out, "How can we fill a riverbed from a well?

It seems to me folly!"

The beggar roused and said, "Nevertheless, it is the folly I have given you to do. I have rescued you twice. Do not doubt me for a third time." And he turned again to watch the dry river. His eyes noticed too the two graves lying beneath the thirsty willows.

At the end of an hour, he bade them stop. "Look downstream. Behold the river, and see the fruit of your obedience." They looked, and they saw deep waters swelling from the mud and flowing eastward away. "You may stop now, for you have repaid the blessing. You should harvest your fields at once, for the snows are not far behind me.

"And do this: Keep one bucket full of this water, and place it on the altar of the Elder God. There the sun will not dry it, nor will the birds come and drink of it. When your harvest is nearing an end, and you have need of more water than your well gives you, take that water and pour it into the river. It is my gift to you. But do not use it until your wells are low and you have need of much water for the harvest. Then this river which is the life of your grain will flow for you again. Go. Your fields are calling."

Covenant watched them go, and then turned to Wordsmith. "This gentle flood will reach the other village this night. There it will swirl through thirsty fields, reviving, ripening."

"You need say nothing more," said Wordsmith. "The river speaks for you."

FOURTEEN

A
Price
of Tears

STALLS OF MERCHANDISE LITTERED THE WINDING STREETS of Glory—women and men selling cloth, fruit, meat, and jewelry, competing for the attention of the hordes. Unlike the other merchants, who shouted the praises of their goods and jostled for attention, Wordsmith stood patiently as all of Glory streamed by. In and atop a box on a wooden table before him were a handful of books, no two the same. Some were small, some large, some thick, and some thin.

Few browsed, but one man lingered and looked. "This is a handsome book," he said at last, pointing to the most ornate of all Wordsmith's wares. "How many coins will it cost me?"

"Coins cannot buy it, nor will I give it away," answered Wordsmith. "It was written with weeping, and I paid a price of tears for every word. And as I cannot sell it for less than it cost me, the price to you is also a price of tears."

"What foolishness is this? Do you take me for one who mourns at will, or for a fee? This whole world is not worth a tear!"

"This whole world is worth much more than a tear—it is worth blood. But you are not ready to understand that either. Yet this book is to be yours someday; it was written for you." Wordsmith opened the book and pointed to the inscription inside.

"It has my name in it!" exploded the man. "What sort of sorcerer are you?"

"I did not know of myself that your name was Ellard, though I myself wrote it there. It was told to me by someone who does know. You see, some books are written for the many, some for the few, and a handful for one reader alone. This book was written for you—but you may not claim it until the full price has been paid."

The man stood bewildered as Wordsmith continued. "You have many other books already."

"Many—as some count many," the man countered. "Perhaps not so many as I would count them. But what I have are exceedingly fine and difficult to come by. All have been made with care. They are works of love that bring delight at every viewing."

"But you speak only of the bodies of books. What of their souls? What of the truths they contain?"

"Some of the books must contain great wisdom indeed," the man said, "for the words are so high and flowing that I scarcely understand what they could mean."

"Then they probably are not true. The truth is easy to see, and it is not hard to understand, though it is often very hard to accept." Wordsmith pointed again to the book in his hand. "But even so, these words would be utter foolishness if you were to read them now, for you would not yet understand why they must be written, or why anyone would need with all their aching heart to read them." Wordsmith set the book down on the table, along with the others. "Go away for now. But come back to me, without fail, when you have learned to grieve. When your heart has been broken, and your hopes are gone, you will be ready. Then and only then shall you have this book."

Ellard went away seething, yet wondering greatly at the ways of the man with the cryptic sayings.

Wordsmith continued to display his books to the unheeding crowd until the hot sun thinned the streets of people.

That same night, Wordsmith was in the highest room in Covenant's house when the earth trembled for a score of heartbeats. Throughout Glory, dishes toppled and walls warped. In one part of the city, a house fell in upon itself and perished in flames sparked by the fire on the hearth.

Wordsmith watched from the window in his tower study and descended the long stairs seeking Covenant's face. "Is this the disaster you have spoken of?" he asked urgently.

"It is," answered Covenant. "Come, we have a visit to make. Woebearer has already gone where he is needed; call Candle and ask him to come with us."

Together the three traversed the streets of Glory, winding their way toward the scene of destruction. They came to the place where the restless earth had brought the great house to its ruin.

"This is where Ellard lives," said Covenant, as the three mingled with the gathering crowd.

"Until this evening he did," added Wordsmith. "No one can live here now."

One man knelt close before the ruins, gazing in anguish at the rubble, blood staining his hands and face. Two children lay crumpled in the dirt at his feet. The buzzing crowds held back, but Wordsmith and Covenant approached and knelt beside Ellard.

"Buildings fall," murmured Covenant, "and belongings

burn. It is not a new thing, and neither is death. Why did you rescue the children and not your books?"

"I do not know," replied Ellard, staring into the final flames with hollow eyes. "They were trapped beneath the bricks. There was no time left before the fire began to spread. Are they dead?"

"No, but they will die if they are not cared for."

"Who are they?" asked Wordsmith.

"I do not know their names," admitted Ellard. "Two urchin brothers who lived in the shadows behind the house. Sometimes I gave them scraps from my table."

"They have no one, then?" inquired Wordsmith. "Even though they have been battered by the stones and scorched by the flames?"

Ellard shook his head slowly, unaware that Covenant was doing the same.

"You pulled them from the rubble," said Covenant, "and now they are yours. I will give you all food and a place to sleep in my house, but you must care for them yourself."

Wordsmith glanced curiously at Covenant, knowing that a full cure was less than a word away. He began to speak, when Covenant motioned silence with a wave of his hand.

Without further conversation, the two men pulled unburned boards from the wreckage and eased the brothers' prostrate forms onto them. With Wordsmith in front and Covenant trailing, they carried the first boy away. Ellard, still numb with shock, grasped one end of the board and helped Candle bear the second child away.

Woebearer returned after them from the streets, feeling the presence of pain in the house. He found Covenant and pressed him for an explanation. "You have never allowed suffering in this house! Where are they? I must see them at once."

Covenant gripped the hunchback's shoulder and sat him down firmly on the stairs. "Woebearer, my friend, I have given you much and restored your strength nightly. In return I have

asked little of you. Now I ask of you a hard thing, a desperately hard thing. Do not heal the boys. Do not go near them, do not speak to them, do not let their suffering summon you to their side. They are Ellard's burden, and not yours. It is his task to apply herbs and wrappings and soothing words. This is a load you may not yet carry."

Woebearer began to protest, but Covenant cut him short. "Each night you return smiling and suffering to my house; each morning you rise refreshed and unburdened to plunge into the limitless pool of pain called Glory. But have you truly healed? Have you erased the agony and sent it away into the outer darkness forever? No. You have not. You have merely shifted the pain from the shoulders of the sufferers to your own. The mere transfer is noble, but falls far short of destruction and obliteration.

"It is an ugly law: there is no healing without suffering. By the wounds of another we are healed; only if someone suffers for us can we find healing. Pain cannot be undone. It may only be carried by someone else, until it is all destroyed by the one who made possible the pain.

"I heal the outside of you—nightly, and temporarily. When I heal the inside of you, it will be forever. But he who truly heals must drink the bitter brew that tastes like blood and death.

"I have given you this command," Covenant said, "and there is nothing else to say for now. If I thought you would understand the reasons I forbid you, I would tell you plainly. You have more power than you have wisdom. You see suffering as only an evil snake to be snuffed out wherever it is seen. It is a snake and it *is* evil, but it may sometimes be put to good use."

FIFTEEN

Words for the Wounded

ELLARD CAME INTO THE ROOM WHERE WORDSMITH WAS writing. The writer looked up and asked, "How are they?"

"They are not dying," Ellard said. "If their wounds were mortal, they would be dead by now."

"This is the third day."

Ellard nodded. "And I have been at their side for all of them. Mercifully, they have mostly slept and moaned, and not wakened often to the fullness of their agony."

"And your own wound?"

Ellard absently touched the small bandage on his head. "It is nothing."

"It is more than you think. It is the first blood you have shed for the world. Much has changed since first we met in the street," observed Wordsmith. "You have lost your old loves and gained new ones."

"I did not know the children, for I did not care for them. But by caring for them, I have come to know them. In knowing them, I find that I am beginning to love them. It is a strange thing."

"You should love them," said a new voice, "for they have cost you dearly." Neither man had seen Covenant enter the room, holding a bag at his side.

"You were not a fool to rescue them," he added quietly. "You would be a fool if, having rescued them at the price of your old treasure, you now turned away from them. If you had tried to save your collected wealth instead of the boys, you would have lost everything: all the books, your house, and your own life as well. Instead, you gave mercy. You shall receive mercy in return."

"Will they live?"

"They will live, and they will need you."

"How can I help? I am no healer."

"You can bring them stories to ease their agony and mend their minds."

"They cannot read."

"True, but they can listen. And to bring them that solace you will need the help of some old friends."

"Old friends?" he questioned. "I have none. All my companions perished with my house."

"Perhaps," said Covenant, "and perhaps not." He reached into the bag at his side and carefully stacked the corpses of a dozen scarred books on the table.

Holding his breath, Ellard took the uppermost volume and cradled it gently in his hand. The binding was torn where bricks had scored it, blackened where flames had scorched it, and swollen where water had dripped upon it. The papers were loose and would ever smell of mold and damp and fire. But all the pages were there.

The others were in similar condition—ruined but not destroyed.

"There are other uses for books than to please eyes and fingers and intellect," said Covenant. "You shall discover another one now. Take this book and read it to the boys. They will wake soon, but they cannot rise; they will need kind words of many kinds. This is a lesson for you: the bodies of these books have been destroyed, although their souls have been spared. I know that wounds you, but I counsel you to consider that *every* body is perishable, though *any* soul may endure."

Covenant left the tower, and Ellard sadly contemplated the remains of his fallen but uncomplaining friends.

"They were, I believe," said Wordsmith, "the only books from your collection that Covenant found of much value."

"But these are all children's tales!"

Wordsmith picked up a battered volume and carefully turned the pages as he answered. "Most likely the rest were full of wind and not wisdom—folly, and not philosophy. They pretended to hold the truth but sheltered only lies instead. These," he said, elevating the book in his hand, "do not pretend to have the truth, and so have many truths in them. You kept them, I think, because of their fine binding. They look as though they were handsome once."

Ellard nodded, genuine tears brimming his eyes.

"You may now discover their true value," added Wordsmith, surrendering the book to Ellard. "You will find that Covenant has a taste for true stories—stories that are always true, stories that once were true, stories that should be true." He smiled before adding, "And stories that one day shall be true."

SIXTEEN

The Hope
of the Healer

AN ANGRY ELLARD, TRAILING WOEBEARER IN HIS WAKE, AT last found Covenant in the house. The beggar was speaking with Wordsmith in the tower. "We have spoken together for the first time, Woebearer and I," Ellard began. "I did not know that you were a healer, or that another healer lived under your roof. Why then have the children been permitted to suffer? Why have you forbidden this man to come to us?"

"For reasons of my own, I have neither healed them nor permitted them to be healed," responded Covenant slowly. "They will hurt, but they will not die." And again, smiling sadly, he walked away, beckoning Woebearer to follow.

"These boys will continue to break your heart," continued Wordsmith, after Covenant and Woebearer had departed. "So Covenant has said. But why it will be better this way, I do not know."

Elsewhere, Covenant said to Woebearer, "Hold your healing. This pain is not yet yours to destroy. It is a cruel thing to say, but sometimes suffering is necessary."

"For the children? What have they to learn?"

"It is necessary for you. I must arrest your gift for a time until you learn that it is not your salvation. Neither is it your burden to the grave. It is a gift. In your belief alone is your salvation. When you see that, you will know that all your wretched burdens have long since been lifted from your shoulders. Know too," Covenant added, "that their suffering is also necessary for Ellard."

And Covenant would say nothing beyond that.

The next day, Ellard confronted Covenant and Wordsmith again. "Why? Why are you letting this go on?" he thundered.

Covenant stood silently, though not without compassion.

"WHY?" screamed Ellard, as tears trickled down the new furrows that had come in recent days to seam his face. "For days now they have been crying for relief, finding none save in my voice."

Covenant turned to Wordsmith and said simply, "Behold his anguish. It is time."

Wordsmith nodded, and Covenant left while the unanswered challenge rang in the air. Wordsmith pulled a thick, richly bound book from his pocket and handed it to Ellard.

"It is yours now. You have earned it, for you have proved the lie of your own words about the worth of the world. When you were crying for your books only, your tears availed you nothing. But I said that you might have this book when you had learned how to grieve. You could not have it before this, for you had failed to understand the heart of books, though you loved them. Your eye was enchanted by the binding, and not by the truth of the words within."

That night, as the boys finally slid into troubled sleep, Ellard read the book silently by the light of the smoking lamp. He kept the words to himself.

Long before the dawn, Ellard sought Covenant but could not find him. Wordsmith was at hand, still awake and writing, and eager to speak with him.

"Have you finished the book yet?" Wordsmith asked.

"Yes," said Ellard slowly, as if still half in a dream. "I came to the end of the book but not the story. It ends in the middle of a sentence . . . rather painful, even, for I so wanted it to go on and on and on with never an end, and I do wonder what happened."

"Perhaps you will be granted a glimpse of the knowledge of the rest of the story, though you will never come to the end. It is a true story with never a final chapter."

"The words were new to me, but the story stirred ancient memories." He spoke tenderly, choosing his words carefully, a faraway look in his eyes. "I must have heard it a long time ago—so long past I can scarcely remember."

"It is an old story," Wordsmith nodded with a smile, "and the greatest one of all. There will never be a time when that tale is not remembered, recounted and enjoyed."

"I cannot believe that you, a mere man, wrote those words."

"I did indeed write these words, but they are only echoes of the tales from a book that Covenant keeps hidden away. I have seen that book and would lose my life to save it if it were necessary. But it will not be necessary, for it is the book that saves me and not I the book. That book cannot be spread abroad yet. Someday, all people everywhere will know its stories by heart. Until then, I am permitted to write ghost echoes of its beauties, to draw people to Covenant and this house."

Wordsmith wandered to the window, and a long silence came to dwell in the room. It endured until Covenant appeared.

"Do you still demand that they be healed?" Covenant asked Ellard directly.

"No," he said finally, with a mixture of resignation and peaceful enlightenment. "I see now that there are other matters that matter more. Thank you for the book. It is the first book I have ever held whose soul was more beautiful even than its body."

"You have long kept books, but now this book will keep you. And so I rename you as I have renamed almost every person in this house of mine. You shall be known as Binder. And I think such a book as you now have should be read to your charges—the sooner the better. This will be the best of all medicines for them, as it has been for you. It is fit that they hear it first from your lips."

Binder obeyed, and sought his suffering friends.

*   *   *

Later, at the midday meal, Covenant found Woebearer and Wordsmith and nodded to the hunchback. "You may go to them now," he said simply. And food forgotten, Woebearer sprang away like a honed arrow to its mark.

After a moment, Wordsmith asked, "Was all this delay truly necessary?"

"It was," said Covenant. "Someday you will see the secret purpose behind all mysterious things. Come."

They followed Woebearer's footsteps and came to the room where the children lay. The sound of laughter spilled from the room. Binder and the boys embraced, and Woebearer embraced them, and then Covenant embraced them all. Although there were more new lines carved into Woebearer's brow, he did not seem to notice.

"Their pain is gone now," said Covenant when the laughter subsided to joyful smiling. "But their strength will return only over many days. There are still stories they have never heard."

"But I have no more books—and no more stories!" protested Binder. "I have read them every word of this wonderful volume, but they do not seem to understand it."

"Perhaps it is because this book was written for you," replied Covenant. "Perhaps they shall understand it when they are older."

"That is why we shall be good friends," said Wordsmith. "I write books, and you read them. It is such an excellent combination. You may read more of my stories to them, and then it will be time to create your own and write them down. Then you will have the privilege of learning the true delight of books. For I have found that the one who writes a book learns more than the one who reads it."

The weariness of relief swept through the room. What had once been sleepless pain became painless sleep for the boys.

The four men stood quietly by and watched them slumber.

"They are much alike," said Binder.

"Their two hearts beat as one," answered Covenant. "They will not be stopped in anything they do. In fact, they barely will be guided." And Covenant blessed them, calling good fortune and honor down upon their heads. And at that moment, he named them Firecolt and Flamerider. "You have always been together," he whispered to them. "Never shall you be parted—in this world or the next."

— SEVENTEEN —

Beauty
& the
Feast

BEAUTY HAD KNOWN FAME, REWARD AND THAT WHICH WAS said to be love. And then in the space of a summer she had faded from splendor as the masses turned their attentions to another who was fresher and more fair.

Now she wandered alone through the places where once she had gathered crowds; weary and sleepless where once she had the offer of a hundred beds; rejected and forgotten in the midst of the congregation that once had mouthed her praises.

Beauty heeded not her footsteps until she raised her eyes and saw before her a pair of gates she did not recognize. The gates stood open, and the road beyond beckoned with a peculiar urgency. She followed the path into the sandy wilderness of the desert, content for now in the knowledge that the great town could do nothing but dwindle behind her back.

One mile beyond the gates the road divided, arching away to the left and the right. A high flat rock slumbered in the notch of the fork, and two men sat on the rock. The man on the left was tall and fair, cloaked in white silk unsullied by the dust of the earth. His skin was smooth and lightly tanned, like many of the high gentlemen she had known. The man on the right was neither short nor tall, neither young nor old, and his beggar's coarsecloth was marked with the dust of the highways and the darker, thin grime of the unwashed streets. His work-gnarled hands and lined face had long been bronzed and cracked by the sun.

Both men seemed to be waiting for her. She stopped and stared uneasily at them. She dimly remembered their faces, seeing for a brief instant the images of two men standing against one another on a wretched side street.

The gentleman spoke first. "You are a long way from home."

She nodded, looking up. "It is my choice. I leave it behind of my own free will." The sound of her own voice encouraged her.

"And why? Where would you go instead? Is not this town the center of all the world?"

"I have lost the fame that was mine. Perhaps I will find it again in another place which does not count itself so civilized. Or perhaps I will find the City, if indeed it exists. Some say it lies this way, or that, and that one may find pleasant things there."

"Who are you to seek these things?"

"My name is Beauty. Who are you?"

"I am Fame. I am the Master of all that is glorious. Honor and Fortune are my servants."

Then the beggar spoke. "I have many names. You may call me Covenant."

"Is that your true name?"

"All my names are true."

Fame spoke again. "How fortunate that you have come to me in your seeking. The City, indeed, lies before you—there!" He pointed down the road to the left, and Beauty thought she saw the way straight and golden, with tall towers and bright banners at its faraway end. He dropped his hand, and the vision faded into the shimmer that always bathes the desert horizon. "The way is open and needs only your feet upon it."

The beggar broke in. "That way is an illusion, and the path a snare. The true way to the true City lies through the very heart of the town you have abandoned. I have set a man there to guard the way and hold the key to the door. If you wish to find the City, you must return and find the man who serves me.

"To go onward leads only to the realms of Fame. Beyond this rock that road is one way, leading not to the City but to desolate lands that have long forgotten the sun. Fame sits here, guarding not the path beyond but the way back.

"His kingdom is made of false towers," Covenant added, "with hollow lands behind. The grand gate at the base of the towers is the Doorway of Deceit. Return with me to the town and the City within. Fame lays a trap for you, and all other quests are in vain."

Fame interrupted him, shaking his head. "The foolish words of a beggar. He offers you nothing. I offer you love. How many husbands have you had?"

"Five. No, six."

"I can promise you many more—husbands, or at least men to love you freely."

Covenant spoke again. "A worthless gift that will leave you as unfilled and aching as you already are. I offer you the hope of only one man—if he chooses to have you, and you him. A man who is mine and changes not from day to day, except that he is free to respond to those who have need of him."

"What manner of offer is that?" countered Fame. "I give you a feast! Wine, song, laughter, crowds, honor."

"But I offer you a different Feast. Food for your spirit. A song for your soul. The laughter that heals the heart. The company of a few. And the honor of serving one who serves a holy cause."

Fame's hands moved in the air, as though stroking Beauty's face. "And what of the glory of your face? The flesh! So easy to mold—a touch here, a stroke there, and you will be more striking than any the world has yet seen. Your first beauty was your own and was mortal, but what I give you shall be unearthly. All will fall anew at your feet. You shall be high and lifted up, and men shall once more fight to serve you."

Covenant's eyes met her own. "I give you not beauty re-newed but the knowledge of yourself, and a new chance to be what you might have been had your beauty not hindered you. The one who serves me shall give you leave to serve him; he shall not lift you up, but you him, and he will give you honor but not worship."

Fame countered, "You have tasted fading glory in a place that will also fade. Do you desire eternal fame?"

The beggar interrupted. "He offers you eternal *flame*. Do not listen to him. All his words sound too like one another. His words build a grand illusion—and a fatal one, for his touch brings decay."

She wept. "You confuse me," she said, shaking her head and turning away. "Both of you—go away and let me be."

Jumping down from the rock, Covenant answered her with quick yet gentle words. "No. That we cannot do, for you have come to us and must walk one or the other of the ways that we guard." He pointed to the left, while peering into Beauty's eyes. "His road leads without turn to his own realms, and my road turns here upon itself to lead you back through the town." He gestured to the right.

"Can this Fame do what he promises?" she asked. "Can he return to me all that was mine?"

"He can restore to you—for a time—the illusion that you

had when you claimed those things for your own. I offer you more, but you will not know it now. I offer you the loss of all you hold dear and the gain of all you think you never wanted. You are empty, because you have already lost. Do not seek to retain what you cannot keep." He paused. "You are tired, and I shall bring you to a place to sleep. The house of Wordsmith is open to you this night, if you will come."

"Wordsmith? I think I have heard that name."

"You have," Covenant said, gently reaching his arm around her shoulders. "And you have laughed at him. Wordsmith is his name now, but he was not born with it. He was a great man once, as some reckon greatness. But I claimed him, and he took my yoke upon him and became mine. He accepted the fire of my refining, the piercing of my breaking him—and gave up all he once had. Now he sits alone, and sees far visions, and thinks hard thoughts, and writes the unchanging words that I put in his heart, and serves a Feast daily. His words and his service have spread farther than his fame. You were given some of his writings, but they gathered dust on your costly shelves, and you did not heed the weight of his words. It would have been better for you if you had."

She blinked away the last of the tears from her eyes and looked up to the rock again—catching Fame in the last split-second of an ugly scowl. It had not been directed at Covenant alone, but at her as well. It was gone in a heartbeat, replaced by the smile that now seemed so false.

Covenant looked at her, knowing what she had seen. "This is my way," he said. "Any who stand by me long enough come to see the truth behind everything."

On an impulse she would question many times but never regret, she dismissed Fame with the wave of her hand. Then she followed Covenant silently back along the beggar's road to the town cloaked in twilight.

They passed through Glory's gates again and journeyed past the places she had abandoned, past the entertainment halls, and past the places where the people crowded together noisily. They left the torchlights behind them and wound their way deeper into the older and shabbier districts of the town, between the buildings where rats rustled and children cried and the buildings themselves towered ominously in the darkness. There in the very heart of the squalor they stopped before a door. Covenant bade her sound the knocker. Then he left her.

When the door opened, the gift of speech was taken from her, and Beauty stood mute and frightened and needy on the doorstep. Wordsmith drew her inside, gently, and his face showed no surprise. *His words have always borne fruit,* thought Wordsmith, *but I never know when to expect a harvest.*

The door closed behind her, and her helplessness rolled over her in thrashing waves. Weak, hungry and weary, she could no longer find the strength to bolster courage, the fierceness to defend herself, the power to resist, the voice to question or cry out. She was in the hands of Wordsmith, for good or for bad, both vulnerable and dependent. She trembled, and he soothed her with a word and led her to a table laid for a meal. It looked as though many others had recently eaten there, yet there was food in abundance. He held his hands out, palms downward, and proclaimed a blessing.

She sat, and ate with a hunger she could no longer conceal. The food was excellent and plentiful, and the very act of eating increased her desire. Wordsmith moved slowly about elsewhere in the house; she heard the faint sounds of doors opening and closing and water gurgling from stone jars.

When she finished, he led her to a place where a bath was drawn, and left her. She bathed and dressed herself in the new clean coarsecloth lying there. Then Wordsmith came again and led her to a room where a bed stood freshly made. And she grew sad inside, expecting to pay for his kindness with her favors. But Wordsmith only bade her good sleeping and left her alone. She slept, unaware that he returned in the middle of the night with more blankets, or that he stood long in the

doorway and gazed at her, wondering what manner of woman slept within her.

For two days she lingered speechless in the house, sharing with open eyes the Feast given daily by Wordsmith—plain banquets opened to the homeless, the hopeless, the destitute discards who crowded in hungrily to the laden table, yet who showed their respect for the master of the house.

She discovered many things that she did not understand— doors that would not open to her, doors that she could not shut, staircases that had no landing and no end, mirrors that reflected nothing or frightened her when she looked into their depths. And though the door to the street opened freely at her touch, yet she stayed. If any had asked, and if she had possessed the voice to answer, she would have said that she stayed of her own will and choosing.

And she came to see what she had not noticed the first night: Wordsmith was lame, though he moved with slow grace and did not always use a walking stick.

On the morning of her third day in the house, the freedom of her tongue returned to her. She came first to Wordsmith and thanked him for his kindness, asking him why she had received so much care and yet so little had been demanded of her.

"Why should I ask anything of you?" he answered, laying aside his work. "I am here to serve Covenant."

"Why do you keep this house and serve this feast? Who are you, and who is Covenant? I have met you both, but I know neither of you."

"This is not my house," he said, waving her to a chair. "It is Covenant's. This world is Covenant's. He walks unseen here. It is his Feast that I serve here, to the people whom he has touched with his care. I am his servant, his anointed houseman. He it was who turned me from the greed of the world, from the worship and celebration of things that perish, from the living of a life that held no promise but unholy fame."

And Wordsmith told Beauty the tale of the night he had met Covenant—of the dusty beggar held for the death and burial of an old worthless man who was needed only for the grinding of the harvest—of a verdict of death, of the fire that could not be kindled and the greater fire that could not be quenched.

"I lived in Glory once," he said, "and left it behind me because of all the falseness and misery."

"I too have known misery. Has Covenant changed Glory, that you can live in it now?"

"No. He has changed me that I might live in Glory. He promised me that—and his name is Covenant because he keeps his promises."

She motioned to the room in which they sat. "But why is this house here?"

"Of fourth importance, it is a house for Covenant's servants.

"Of third importance, it is a house of healing for those who suffer from the sickness unto death, the wounds that come from the weight of a world broken upon its own altar.

"Of second importance, it is the place where a Feast is laid daily for any who will come.

"But this is the first meaning of this house: Behind a door in this house is the path to the City."

Her heart jumped at his words, but he continued before she could speak. "That is why Covenant turned your feet from the path that is drifted deep with the dust of death. Your eyes were blinded, as they always have been. Even now you see only dimly, as though you peer into a mirror never cleaned and never purged of old, deceptive images.

"The door to the path to the City lies behind you," he continued, nodding toward the long corridor. "And Covenant bade me show you the way whenever you desire."

"Yes, please! Even now!" She left the chair tilted behind her and caught herself at the door.

"You may go if you choose," he said, "for there is none to

stop you except yourself. But hear my words first."

She turned and looked at him.

"I do not advise that you go to the City now," he said. "You could not stand there unaided, or withstand the weight of joy unrestrained by sorrow. Remember that as there are lights too bright to see by and sounds too loud to hear, so there are glories too high and lovely to behold with unredeemed eyes. And redemption lies only in this house.

"The bright shadow of the City is here in this town, if you would but see it. Do not go to the City now. Not yet. Linger here instead—tarry, stay, enjoy—and learn to both see and endure the lesser glories before you expose yourself to the Life of the City, which is health and nectar to those who have both the desire of a new heart and the endurance of courage renewed. It is overwhelming pain to those who have neither."

"I am ready to journey now. I have seen too much of this town," she said, gesturing to the streets beyond the window.

"So you think. Perhaps you have not seen enough. But go, if you will. I will open the door for you, and Covenant will meet you along the way." He led the way through the winding halls to a door in one of the walls—a door she had tried on her own once before. It had been a door that she could not open, a door that should have opened into the back of another room. The hand-hewn wood bore ancient marks in odd places, and she could not name the dark stains lying deep in the grain.

"The path will turn long among the mountains," Wordsmith said, "and darkness will rise up to surround you. But the sky is clear, the morning star will guide you, and you will see a few steps before you and a few steps behind. You will be frightened, but you cannot be harmed. And then . . . then, you will come to the peak and see the City before and above you, and the night will be forgotten. If the City draws you gently, but the rush of beauty and holiness does not break your heart, then you should go farther. Journey on until your heart remembers its early thirsts.

"But when you have drawn close enough and your soul is suddenly drawn with the raging thirst that can only be quenched by the waters in the fountains before you—then return to me, for you will have motive enough and memory sufficient to aid me in my work here." He saw that Beauty hesitated. "Go on, go on," he urged, "and gaze upon the City. Fear not. The path from here is steep but certain. The hard part, the perilous way, is to return in obedience."

"I shall not return," she stated flatly.

"If you do not return, I shall understand, and all will be well. If you do return, I shall also understand, and all will be better."

He opened the door with a twist of his key and by speaking Covenant's name. She looked through the archway upon a path winding among tall mountains under an endless starry sky.

*　　*　　*

Wordsmith was preparing the table for the evening Feast when Beauty slipped softly into the dining hall. She nested silently in one of the chairs and gazed at him. Not all the tears had dried from her face.

He ceased his labors and drew a chair near to hers. "Words are painful now, I well know. I will not ask you to speak. But I will tell you how it was.

"You saw the City, did you not? And Covenant met you on the way?"

She nodded.

"How well I remember," he said. "To see the City is to seal one's desire to dwell there. But it is not like any earthly desire. It is not a consuming passion that one feels must be filled at once, before all else, without reckon of the cost. No, it is certain, safe, durable, everlasting. And most who see it are content to return here, to abide, to serve faithfully the beggar who is himself faithful to the High King of the City." He paused, searching her face. "Did Covenant ask you to return?"

She nodded again.

"He did not command you?"

This time she shook her head.

"And you do so willingly? To serve me as I serve him?"

Another nod.

Wordsmith nodded with her. "Once one sees how solid is the City, one is content to do other things first. Come. I accept your service, as he accepted mine. Aid me with this table now, and tomorrow I shall teach you the inner ways of this house."

EIGHTEEN

The Marvelous Mirror

ONE DAY BEAUTY FOUND THE NURSERY. SHE LINGERED long there, fascinated by the odd mixture of infants and ancients. A dozen old men and women happily tended to a noisy gathering of babies; some fed and changed their charges, some played on the floor, and some too frail to move about simply sat and held the small ones. All looked worn by time, but not defeated by the demands of their children.

Trueteller was among them, holding a baby on each arm and talking to a young man on whose face a glorious tawny beard had begun to blossom. He, too, rocked a child firmly but gently in his arms. They did not see Beauty, and she did not distract them as she left.

"Lionheart is the father of them all," smiled Covenant. "Though they had many fathers, now they have only one.

Young and old alike were betrayed, and now he has brought them together to mingle the old wisdom with the young innocence."

"I do not understand. Where did they come from? Why is he called Lionheart?"

"That story should come to you from his own lips."

Later, she asked more questions of Wordsmith, but all he would say was "Covenant's advice is good—for Lionheart, too, is a good storyteller, and he is a very patient man."

She thought for a moment, and then asked, "Why do all of you stay?"

"Our work here is founded upon the power of paradox," Wordsmith said. "We who keep this house have all seen the City. Even as our desire grows to journey on, the more our strength and yearning grow to serve Covenant here."

"I shall serve as well," she declared. "Where do I begin?"

"At the beginning—as we do each day." He led her into the long hall beyond the Feast table. "Have you seen this mirror?"

"Yes! I despise it, for I looked into it when first I came here. It showed me horrid things."

Nevertheless, fascinated, she raised a finger to stroke its intricate frame.

"It showed you only yourself as you were. It is not a mirror that has been fashioned by hands of this world. It is Covenant's command that we each stand daily here, alone, and see ourselves without pretense in its glass."

She looked, and beheld herself as a hideous, twisted, weak creature—grotesque and hardly human, defiled and deformed. She cringed and turned away from Wordsmith. "That is not me! It cannot be!"

"The mirror does not lie," he said. "Look again, for you have not seen enough."

She looked again, fearfully, and saw this time that hideous reflection swathed in a robe the color of new snow. She turned to Wordsmith in wonder.

"Look again," he gestured with a broad smile. "There is more."

She looked yet one more time, but now she saw Covenant's face beside hers in the glass. She felt his arms join around her waist and heard his voice soft in her ear. She laughed, basking in the flood of sudden warmth. Somewhere deep inside her she heard a sound like old frozen chains shattered by a great flame.

"Wordsmith! He loves me anyway!" The radiance of the embrace faded, and the mirror shaded into featureless gray.

"Yes. And that is the mystery. We must be reminded daily of both our low stature and his high love. Our answers lie only in Covenant and his choices."

They walked slowly into the kitchen.

"Then our work begins," he continued. "We need food for the Feast, and today you will gather it for us."

"Where do I buy it? For how much? And with what?"

"You do not buy, neither will you beg, or steal. You must go, and wait; be found, and receive. Take this basket and walk through the streets of the town. Do not hail those you know—if indeed any of your former friends would recognize you in these common clothes. Wait, hurry slowly; tarry, but do not stand still. Covenant has prepared the hearts of some to see you, to give you food and fruit out of their abundance. Take, accept without question. Do not test the quality of what is given you. Count not the outward appearance, but bring all of it here when the basket is full, and bless it in your bringing. Covenant shall then make the one basket suffice." He picked up a large, sturdy, but well-worn basket. "Do not speak, do not multiply your thanks, but bow gracefully and move on. We do not walk the same path twice in a week, nor the same path on the same day of each week."

"It all sounds so . . . uncertain."

"So it is, in our eyes. But not in his." He gave her the basket. "Go now, and return when the basket is full."

She paused at the door and turned back. "Will you not go with me?"

"Not today. There is no need, for there is nothing to risk but your pride, and nothing to lose but your independence. You walk under the protection of Covenant, for your work is done in his name. And for the time that you are away, he has given me other work to do. When you return, seek me on the topmost floor at the end of the farthest stair."

Beauty stepped outside and carried the empty basket away into the swarming town.

NINETEEN

The Five Windows

BEAUTY STOOD AT THE FOOT OF THE STAIRS AND GAZED upward. These were the stairs that had frightened her when she had first tried them, for they seemed without landing and without end. But she ascended, and somewhere on the heights Wordsmith heard her footsteps and came to meet her.

"You did well," he said.

"How do you know? You were not with me!"

"Ah, but in a way I was. Come, see the secrets of this upper room." He drew her up the last steps into a room with five great windows. Four of the windows peered out over the town—four windows glazed with clear crystal that offered no reflection.

"From here one can see everywhere within the town—and beyond. Look there: It is the road you followed to your meeting with Covenant—and the road by which you returned."

She peered through the window, seeing a far road and the flat rock dwarfed by distance. Then it grew closer and larger, until she saw the stone seat as though it were only a pace away. She turned to look at another window, and when she looked back the first view had once more receded into the distance.

"This is how I knew your basket to be full," he said. "One who stands here may watch closely anything he or she desires." He turned her to the fifth window, which until now had been featureless and gray, like storm clouds brooding at dusk. "This is my appointed station," he said. Then the gray faded and a field of stars unfolded like flowers before her. Galaxies gleamed in the sable sky. Comets whirled through blooming constellations.

"Behold the Fields of Arbol—the realm and handiwork of the Elder God." Then the stars were gone, replaced with a glen deep within the center of a green and peaceful forest.

"This is Covenant's window, even as this is Covenant's house. He built this window for me with his own hands. It was his gift to me that I may do the writing he bids me do." The forest faded, and, within the opening, colored shadows shifted and swirled in quiet glory. "I recline here, upon this couch, and watch the visions come and go. And when I have seen them, I fashion them into stories and put them into books. Then I go to the marketplaces and the corners and other towns, and I place my books where they belong, and tell these stories, speaking always of Covenant and the City, and inviting all who will both hear and hearken to come to the Feast.

"Look into the window, Beauty, and see a story for your eyes. I cannot tell you what we will see, but what Covenant reveals here is intended to help you."

The whirling colors ceased their play, and Beauty saw a woman descending steep unlit paths to a dark and sprawling castle where shadows lay like rancid filth in the passageways.

False towers framed the open gates, and every winding stairway led downward to the same deep dungeon.

"That is you, as you might have been," Wordsmith explained. "And those are the realms of Fame. You saw them once, as Fame showed them. Now you see them through Covenant's eyes."

She covered her face with her cloak and the view vanished. "But you are secure now. You need only stay to be redeemed." Soft silence fell as he stared at the window. "Too long have I neglected the tasks of watching, hearing, and writing so that I might bring order to the Feast. I ask you to free me from the kitchen's burdens that I may linger here. There are many sleepless nights, long midnights when the window scrolls and speaks ceaselessly, without regard for the sands of time, hours when I will be grateful for any food or drink you may bring me, and for any weight you may lift from my shoulders. Mine is a lonely task; you cannot join me in it, yet, you can be my solace and my company."

"I will," she said. And then she added, "For once, I have no shame in giving another my service."

They turned away from the window.

"Wordsmith?"

"Yes?"

"If Covenant has healed so many . . . why has he not healed you?"

"When he summoned me, he made my healing no part of the bargain. And it was many months before I grew wise enough to understand his wisdom. Covenant took from me my old name, my old songs and tales, and he gave me new ones instead. He has left me my lameness to remind me of what might have been—to grant me a humbling affliction—to prevent my exaltation in my own eyes.

"He is sufficient now, though I did not see it then. Not all ills are cured by making the body whole. I have seen Covenant heal a broken kitten, yet he has not healed me—at least on the outside. His surgery began quietly on the inside. Someday it may conclude with fanfare on the outside."

"Then who *is* Covenant?"

"Covenant is but one of his names. It is his true name, but it does not contain him. No single name can. In some places he is known only as the Beggar, even though he rises higher than the King. But he is not famous, except among those who have tested all other champions and found them lacking. He comes to those who call for him and to those who do not even know their need of him. Women wake to find sick children well. Poor husbands rouse to find gold beneath their pillows. Starving towns turn and find new fields of grain. The thirsty claim water in his name. The desperate find rest in his hands. The hungry come to his Feast at his invitation. It is he who provides the food, though you carried it. It is his generosity that sparks other hearts to grant the food, and his voice that woos other souls to come and partake of the gifts."

He led her away down the steps to the kitchen, where the unready Feast awaited the touch of her hands. He continued speaking as they walked. "He breaks the proud and shatters unworthy gods. He casts down the prayers of people who seek high things for low reasons. He orders the rainfall and draws the lightning. All these things are from Covenant, and through him, and he comes in the name of the Elder God. Let your own heart tell you who Covenant is—who he must be, who only he can be."

As Beauty worked in the kitchen, she knew as she portioned out the food that none could name it good. Yet the ragged guests at the Feast seemed not to notice. Some tarried after to speak with Wordsmith, and some slipped away into the murky streets, while others stayed to sleep in tiny rooms that opened from the side halls.

After the Feast, Wordsmith took her to meet the others she had seen working in the house, doing other tasks. They all made Beauty welcome, and she was both comforted and, yet, disappointed. There still was something within her that cried out for recognition, but she stood relieved that none spoke to her of her past.

In the evening she tended Wordsmith before his window and watched with him. After the window had paled to gray, they talked until the new day was born.

"Is Wordsmith a true name? Or Woebearer? Your names do not seem proper."

"Covenant gave us our names. Our old names died with our old lives."

"He has not given me a new name," she said simply.

"You have already abandoned the name first given you—and the one you have adopted suits you well enough for now. The best names, the true names, are not yet ready to be revealed. Someday we will hear them from Covenant's own lips."

After that, the time passed in pleasant cycles of hard work and deep sleep, of Covenant coming and going like sunshine through the rainbow and wind across the grass. Again and again Beauty sat with Wordsmith in the marketplace, hearing his tales and teaching, and turned to help him in the long evenings, bringing him food before he asked. Sometimes she wrote down for him the words he chose to fit the visions, and sometimes she simply listened to his wisdom.

"Wordsmith?"

"Yes?"

"It is an odd thing—I am more of a queen here, serving, than in all those houses past where I was served. And I did not know love, although I heard the word often, until I came beneath your care. Yet you have never sought to touch me or fed me sweetened words."

"There is much honor in this house. It falls on all who are humble enough to lay it aside. Do not seek it and it will be given to you."

"It is fortunate for me that you do not see me in the mirror.

Could you do so, or had you seen me so that first night, you would turn me away."

He turned to stare at her for a long moment. "Did not Covenant tell you?"

A puzzled look creased her brow.

"I did see you as you are in the mirror. And I still do. But I also see the white-robed lady with the radiant face. It is like seeing thrice with a single glance—the one inside, the one outside, and the one waiting to be revealed. This way of seeing is one of the gifts he gives the ones who serve him long."

Shame and wonder flooded her soul and peered out through her eyes. "And still you took me in?"

"Certainly. I had no reason to turn you away." He paused, and then continued in softer tones. "Do not forget that I, too, stood before the mirror with a naked heart. And what I beheld there was a foulness you will never approach. You were vain. I was evil. But I will not judge you now. You must judge yourself before him and then accept his judgment."

"Might I someday stand with you at the mirror, then? I would like to see you as you will be."

"If Covenant so grants. Until he allows otherwise, the reflections in his mirror are a private vision."

"The reflections. Wordsmith, it also seems—and perhaps I deceive myself—that when I look into the mirror each day I am less foul than the day before. Is my . . . beauty . . . returning?"

"Yes, some of it. Some of it is merely the dirt coming away. But do not misunderstand—its source is not in you. It is because you dwell in the very shadow of the City, and because Covenant loves me, and I in turn love you. Other men gave you love because you were beautiful; here, you are beautiful because you are loved."

Now answered, she left him to his appointed vigil.

TWENTY

Old Promises

Beauty was eyeing a spot on her cloak when Word-smith found her.

"Wordsmith?" she asked. "I cannot clean this cloak any longer." She dropped the fold back into its place and eyed Wordsmith's cloak. "Why is yours always so clean? And the others' clothing as well?"

"I know the answer to that mystery," said Wordsmith, "but I do not pretend to understand it. The cloak you wear is fine indeed, but it is the one you wore when you left Glory for the wilderness. It is Covenant's wish that, when you realize the poverty of your old clothing, you make a new garment for your own—as all in this house have done."

"I do not know how to sew."

"You can learn. The rest of us have done so before you—

behold my own creation!" She looked more closely at his cloak. "I did not choose the pattern," he continued, "or find the material, but my stitches hold it together. It is good enough for now; I am working on a second cloak which will be better. Then I will unsew this one and refold the cloth and leave it for another to use."

"But how does it stay so clean? I have seen dirt upon it at one hour, and the next the stains have disappeared—and you have not had time to clean it."

"That is because it has been made from Covenant's cloth and then scrubbed upon the rock in the river," replied Wordsmith. "And you must do the same with yours when you have finished."

"I don't understand," she said. "It is winter, and the river is not only filthy but frozen."

Although she did not comprehend, she began to piece and sew with the fabric he brought her. As the cloak she wore grew duller and darker and less fit for wear, her new one began to take shape under her fingers.

"This is strange fabric," she said. "It is not any cloth that I recognize."

"A bolt of this was here in the house when Covenant gave me stewardship of it. I do not know where it was made, or how, or by whom, or even what manner of cloth it is. But it is very beautiful, and it is durable if treated properly."

When she was finished, Wordsmith admired her handiwork—clumsy and unpracticed though it was in places—and bade her take it to the river and wash it there.

"But the cloth is not dirty yet."

"If you do not preserve it by scrubbing it upon the rock in the river, it will soon stain and never come clean again. Then your effort will be wasted, and you will have to begin again.

"I would gladly do it for you," he continued, "but this is one thing you must do for yourself. Come, I will walk with you to the river."

By the water he pointed out the rugged rock, crystalled with ice and glittering in the sun.

"I feel foolish doing this," said Beauty.

"You are foolish. But every time you play the fool by obeying Covenant's commands, even though they bewilder you, you become less of a fool than before.

"The river looks dirty and foul to me as well—but it is Covenant's river, and it carries out his wishes when we do the same."

She went, gingerly treading upon the ice and chopping through the frozen crust with a stick to reach the surface of the rock. There she scrubbed her new cloak in the frigid, murky water and pounded it flat again with a stone.

When she picked her way ashore, her fingers were cut and bleeding and blue with cold. "A little of your own blood will not hurt the cloth," said Wordsmith. "Indeed, it will make the seams—the only part which you have made—all the stronger and all the more lovely."

As Wordsmith and Beauty walked back from the river, Covenant came to Woebearer.

"Your body is worn beyond your time," he said to the hunchback. "You have suffered much that was not your agony to begin with."

"I have," answered Woebearer, "but has it been in vain?"

"It has not. You have helped many."

"But now?"

"But now it is time to make you a whole man at last. That I cannot do here in Glory."

Woebearer nodded. "My feelings fight within me. The City will be pleasant."

"More than pleasant—it will be *right*. For the first time in your life, you shall inhabit a world for which you were made."

"When must I leave?"

"Before the sun hides from the world again. I shall leave the time to your choosing, if it pleases you. You may go this very moment, if you desire. You have nothing to do before you go?"

"I cannot leave now—not just yet. I have strength left in my shoulders, and no weight upon them!"

Covenant smiled, and waved his hand toward the waiting streets. "Then go to the streets one last time. Your deeds cannot save you, but neither will they go uncounted."

They all went about their daily work, knowing that only as the sun fell down the sky would Woebearer return from his final reckless swing through Glory, slumping beneath the staggering weight of his collected sorrows.

*   *   *

That evening Beauty had good reason to test her cloth. After helping serve the Feast, she found new stains upon the fabric. She rubbed them with her finger and waited for the marks to go away. When they did not, she sought Wordsmith and showed him the stubborn blots.

"Perhaps," said Wordsmith with a smile, "you should go and ask Covenant about this."

She found the beggar and asked him, "Why will this dirt not come out? Wordsmith said it is magic cloth and will clean itself."

"What dirt? I see no stains here," said Covenant, peering carefully at her cloak.

She looked down again to point, but found nothing to point to and nothing to say, for it was spotless. It looked as fresh as the day she had first been handed the fabric.

"I think you should ask Wordsmith for a fuller answer," Covenant continued. "He knows more than he has chosen to tell you."

She hurried back to Wordsmith and demanded an explanation.

"You have understood most of it correctly," he said. "It is magic cloth—Covenant's own kind of magic—and it does re-new itself. But time will not erase the stains, nor will anything else but one single act remove a smudge: You must only go and see Covenant. The cleansing only comes when we spend time with him."

Her contemplation was set aside by the arrival of Woebearer. They could all hear him dragging himself joyfully down the street. Wordsmith, Binder, Beauty and Candle met him at the door and helped him down the long halls to the ancient wooden door where Covenant stood waiting.

"I cannot walk another step, my friends," said Woebearer. "I have grabbed more griefs than I can bear."

"I knew you would," answered Covenant. "That is why I have come to carry you myself." Covenant aided the crushed man onto his back and opened the door to the City with one hand. They stepped through, and Woebearer looked back at Wordsmith and the others. For the first time in all his life, joy and full pleasure flushed his face and began to reign there.

All in the house slept well that night, not waiting for Covenant to return. But on the following morning, Beauty sought him, realizing suddenly that she had never seen him standing alone—save those times when she desired to speak with him privately. So once again she made her wish, and it was answered when she came into a side room and found him waiting there—patiently sitting as though only Beauty existed and Covenant had all the time in the world for her.

And Beauty asked him, "You told me once that I might have the hope of a man—you called him 'a man who is mine, who changes not from day to day, except that he is free to respond to those who have need of him.' "

Covenant smiled. "I see you have not forgotten my words."

"How could I fail to remember them? Your promises have a life of their own, and my life has a before and an after because you met me at the rock of choosing."

"I know your question. Yes, Wordsmith is the man who is meant to claim you, and it is within his heart to do so. He has not yet spoken, but I have, and I call it not good that he should

be alone. But do not press him, and do not hurry the time. Each moment comes only in its own season."

Then they climbed to the upper room and joined Wordsmith there, and she was content to stand between the two men as they looked out over the length and width of Glory and all the land beyond, as far as the shores of the sea and the mists of the mountains.

It was Beauty who first spied the wan figure on the nearby path leading into the wasteland, and first called out the name of the most recent beauty, the newly dethroned queen of fickle hearts. Fame was already at the rock, waiting to fill the young woman's empty ear with the illusion of promises and the promise of illusions.

Beauty called to Covenant and asked if she might go with him to meet the one who must, as she had once done, choose one or the other of the roads that go on forever. He smiled, and blessed her, and then the two descended together to the place where the outward road divided in the wilderness.